LAURA VOGT (Teufen, 1989) studied Creative Writing at the Swiss Literature Institute in Biel and Cultural Studies at the University of Luzern. Her debut novel, *So einfach war es zu gehen* (2016), featured at the Solothurn Literature Days and PROSOMOVA. In 2022, we published her second novel, *What Concerns Us*, which was originally published as *Was Uns betrifft* (Zytglogge, 2020). *Woman, Idle* is her third novel. In addition to prose, she also writes poetry, plays and journalistic texts. She lives with her family in eastern Switzerland.

CAROLINE WAIGHT is an award-winning literary translator. Her translations include books by Laura Vogt, Caroline Albertine Minor, Ingvild Rishøi, Maren Uthaug, Asta Olivia Nordenhof and Dorthe Nors. Most recently, she was a finalist for the 2023 PEN Translation Award and received a special commendation at the 2023 Warwick Prize for Women in Translation.

Laura Vogt

Woman, Idle

TRANSLATED FROM THE GERMAN
BY CAROLINE WAIGHT

HÉ/OÏSE

PRESS

First published in English in Great Britain in 2025 by
Héloïse Press Ltd
www.heloisepress.com

First published under the original German language title *Die Liegende Frau*
© Frankfurter Verlagsanstalt GmbH, Frankfurt am Main 2023

This translation © Caroline Waight 2025

Cover design by Laura Kloos
Copy-edited by Robina Pelham Burn
Text design and typesetting by Tetragon, London
Printed and bound in Great Britain by CPI Group (UK) Ltd, Croydon, CRO 4YY

ISBN 978-1-7384594-4-5

EU GPSR Authorised Representative
LOGOS EUROPE, 9 rue Nicolas Poussin, 17000, LA ROCHELLE, France
e-mail: contact@logoseurope.eu

swiss arts council
prohelvetia

Published with the support of the Swiss Arts Council Pro Helvetia

DAY ONE

---

8 June

Romi

I'm lying in a room, but which. Everything around me is vague –
blurred planes in outline. Only the digits on the alarm clock are
bright. Six thirteen. I sit up, the notebook at my side. I run the
tips of my fingers over the words I've written, the individual
letters that score furrows in the thin paper. This is Dennis's room.
He's asleep, his breathing calm, unlike my own. Six fourteen.
I have to leave at half past; I can't be late to visit Nora, and I've got
to go home first, to Phil and Leon, back to where I live, the place
I've settled into, still am settling, trying to settle – and I don't just
mean the flat. Our flat. Phil's flat. *His* inheritance, which includes
the kitchen table he was sitting at the day before yesterday, when
I asked, 'Are you still okay with me spending the night at Dennis's
tomorrow?' Quickly, I added, 'I'm away the next few nights as
well, remember?' He raised his shoulders a couple of centimetres
in a shrug, but his eyebrows, thick as brushstrokes above those
bright eyes, didn't move. Before, I would have been sure that
look meant yes. Before, which is to say 102 days ago, when we
were still an *us*: a man, a woman, a child held by the hand and
an embryo we weren't aware of in a womb; *us*: on the verge of
moving to the village, and we went ahead with it, despite it all.
In spite of Dennis, despite how smudged the meanings of the
words had got: monogamy, love, family, *us*.

The letters on the page, my fingers skimming over them;
I pull back my hand, fold them around the hollows of my knees,
let my head sink down; my back: hunched with shame and

guilt. Then another image, always this, always richly coloured: the man, the woman with her pregnant belly and the child are sitting on the sofa in a freshly painted living room, smiling, happy and relaxed.

But the truth is I have never been this woman. What woman am I then? I release my grip, switch on the bedside lamp.

NOTE

Number of days we have lived in the countryside: thirty-seven.
Number of boxes fully unpacked: three.
Pages I have revised since the move (work-related): twenty-three.
New commissions: zero.
Picture books I've read to Leon: twenty, each at least five times.
Days until my thirtieth birthday: thirty-four.
Number of men I love: two.
Number of beds that are just for me: zero.
Still to do: give the publisher a nudge!

The notebook is light in my hands, whether I'm sitting in Dennis's bed as I am now or in mine and Phil's. As though all that had no weight, the numbers, the words, myself. Amazing how a cover curled with damp and three loose staples can even hold the thing together.

'Fine by me,' Phil had said, the day before yesterday.

I studied him – his high forehead, the reddish hair – and his attentive and yet faintly reticent eyes met mine. Nothing about him had changed in the last few months, or so it seemed. Only this slight dullness, this occasional dissolving of his contours: that is new.

'You sure?' I asked.

'We've already talked about everything Dennis-related,' Phil said. 'And your trip to Berlin.'

But Berlin is off, has been since yesterday afternoon. No city break with Nora and Nora's second best friend, Szibilla. Nora isn't well, she's with her mother, and I've got to go, got to get up, put some clothes on. Right now I only want one thing: to lie here three more minutes next to Dennis, in his bedroom with the yellow rug, the armchair, the desk.

I flick forward a page or two in the notebook.

NOTE

A block of flats in the city, a facade viewed obliquely from above. I'm looking through a window tilted open, and at first all I can see are vague shapes, because the light is reflected in the glass. Every now and then I hear a woman laughing from inside the building. Now I see an armchair, a round yellow rug and a big white desk, on which sit three things: a blunt pencil, a Caran d'Ache ballpoint pen and a branded biro advertising PostFinance. I don't notice what's in the far corner until I'm right up at the window: a bed. One hundred and forty centimetres wide, white bedding, and next to it two rugs; I'm in the middle of the room now. A man and a woman are in bed. Body parts plunge underneath the duvet; others emerge: a leg, a head, toes, a bare stomach, a pale breast and hands that reach out for each other; moving closer, I realise: I am the woman lying there, and I laugh out loud and laugh again as I embrace the other body, pull it to me, into myself; that firm, even pressure when he comes, and suddenly I'm about to come as well, I'm coming, close to him and closer, and I can't help laughing – it's fizzing out of me from everywhere as he continues stroking, as though tracing something with his hands across my back and buttocks, until he too forgets and shudders yet again.

I shift perspective once more; I leave the room. I have seen nothing, really, recognised nothing. I'm back to looking obliquely down at the window from the outside, at the front of the house, the darkening sky. Raindrops come loose, although it's still hot. Summer. Sweat.

On the second page, in the bottom right-hand corner, in smaller writing, it says:

'Thinking is a form of feeling; feeling is a form of thinking.'
(Susan Sontag, 1978)

I wrote that down, did I, made a note of it? But when, when was it again, a couple of days ago, on the train, or that morning, next to Dennis? No, in an hour at my desk; no date, no time. Just these words, my words, which stream in every possible direction, like tiny fish in shallow water, distant suddenly from all connection, already out of sight. I turn to the next blank page and write, automatically, as though by merely noting facts, numbers, I can weave a net to catch at least a few of the fish and allow me to examine them.

NOTE

Number of days until the baby comes, according to the gynaecologist: 155.
Number of nights I will spend with Dennis before then, in the building in the city: twenty-two.
Number of hours I will sit on the train today, travelling to the Rhine Valley: one and a half.
Number of days I will stay there, at a hotel (spa hotel??): five.
Number of francs spent on the accommodation alone, money I don't have: nearly five hundred.

But I have to go, to Nora. What I'm hoping: that she will be better soon. That we will truly see each other, properly, despite the distance of the last few weeks. That at last we can tell each other everything. All about the recent months. Nobody knows me better than Nora.

Six twenty-seven. Dennis lies next to me with his arms at his sides, the covers down around his narrow hips. His bare ribs rise and fall, his skin grey in the wan morning light. In three-quarters of an hour I have to be at home, with Leon, eating breakfast with him, packing his things and mine, taking him to Phil's parents. Then I'm gone.

I see numbers, black and bold, 6 − 2 − 7, 6 − 2 − 8, foreseeable implications. I grab a piece of paper. No sooner do I examine it than it crumbles into glittering dust, forms a new number, 217, pulsing neon yellow, 2 − 1 − 7. Saliva gathers in my mouth, my tongue grows and grows, and with the tip of it I touch the numbers one by one. The two and the one are soft and slippery. Only the seven has edges, cutting into my flesh. Something runs down my chin, dripping onto my collarbone. It spills down between my breasts, onto my stomach and further still; I feel a spreading tingle, and I give birth to a seven, and then comes another and another, every colour, vanishing under the covers in the dark. I open my eyes; so, I am that sort of woman. I turn onto my front. A clatter − the alarm clock falls to the floor. Then I hear Dennis's slow breathing. In. Out. In. Out. In. Silence, like 102 days ago, in room 217, when Dennis slept for just an hour, and I watched him all the while.

It's probably a good thing I'm going away, not to noisy Berlin but to see Nora. Leaving things behind me, sorting them out. I'm sure she'll help me. I'm sure, over the next few days, we'll find our way back to one another.

Szibilla

A woman's reproductive organs are the two ovaries, the two fallopian tubes, the uterus and the vagina.

I close the book. First printed 1981, Zurich Educational Publishing. Let it drop next to the deckchair. Through the high glass walls I'm looking straight out at two spruces. Drying away in the heat. Here, inside, it's the warm damp climate of an overheated swimming pool. I wonder if Romi has arrived yet? It's nearly midday. The machine still isn't working. In a minute I'll give the Miele technician a quick call myself. As soon as this stupid period has started. I can't wait until it's all behind me. This miserable pain in my belly. And everything to do with it.

A defective drive mechanism. Just before the bank holiday, too! The way the building handyman shrugged his shoulders yesterday. Casually. All he said was: 'Better get the manufacturer to have a look at that. Might be tricky, though. Getting someone round the same day.'

'But we're a laundry,' I objected, 'a business! Herr Rüttimann will know it's urgent!' The man replied that I was welcome to try, adding that of course I had a good rapport with him.

He'd barely left before I had Romi on the line. Leon screeching in the background. Nora's mother had just called, Romi said. Nora was at hers. She was sick. Nothing bad, but enough to cancel the trip to Berlin. Nora wasn't answering her phone, Romi said, she'd tried to reach her several times. Did I know what was wrong?

As if Romi hadn't had the chance to ask Nora herself over the last few weeks and months. The mountain of laundry in front of me. We needed a plan. Romi thought we should go straight to the Rhine Valley, do it as cheaply as possible. Airbnb? I could already see it in my mind's eye: dingy. Worn. If we were going to do this, I said, then I wanted a hotel. There was one nearby, not far from Nora's mum. A spa hotel, no frills.

'Too expensive!' Romi instantly replied.

'Then I'll cover some of it for you,' I said. And Romi objecting she couldn't let me do that. And me: If we're going to go on holiday, then we're going to do it properly. And Romi: This isn't a spa holiday, this is about Nora! And me: As far as I'm concerned it's both. I desperately need a break. I put some of my mother's money aside for just this sort of thing. And Romi: Is there anybody in the world who *hasn't* inherited money? And me: I'll just quickly check with the hotel now. I'll let you know. Look, I've got a lot on my plate.

To the right of the spruces, there's a clear view of the valley floor. A clutter of buildings, streets, fields. Car roofs in perpetual motion. The distant Rhine: a taut rope.

My team will make it work today, somehow. One washing machine down. There was grumbling yesterday when I announced the extra Saturday shift. I tried to downplay it: it was just one morning, just one cleaner. Two at the most. It was obviously not ideal, I said, I knew that – but what choice did I have? 'We don't want to spread any germs, do we, don't want any deaths on our hands, eh?' Long faces. Irony is a foreign concept to them. Sadly.

At any rate, not the best beginning to a holiday. Although I don't believe Nora is sick in the ordinary sense of the word.

More likely she had to pay a visit 'to the other side', as she calls it. Gathering herself. In silence. No cakewalk. But it's important, to her. And she'll have her reasons for doing it at her mother's house.

There have been hints. Hints that it would happen again. Ever since the three of us met for coffee at Buena Onda. I'm not surprised that Romi didn't notice. It's the usual story: she's too busy. This time with her second pregnancy. She told us how much she was looking forward to it, the baby. Even though she was exhausted all the time. You could see it. She was jittery. She mentioned another man, too, practically in the same breath.

She'd do better just to clear her head. Concentrate at long last on what really matters. On the lives already in existence. Her first child, for example. Her first husband. And trees. On what human beings are doing to this planet. Not this aimless reproduction.

Nora had had her hair freshly cut and dyed. The ruby red above the narrow face lent the appearance of vitality, the boldness of its colour a distraction from her lostness. In conjunction with the whiteness of her skin, it reminded me of van Gogh's *Almond Blossoms in Red*. Nora's hands were like the branches in the picture. Lean. She gestured with them as she spoke. Asking about the trip we were planning to Berlin. That she'd been thinking: what if Romi came along as well? It had been too long, she said, since we'd done something as a trio. And it would do Romi good. A few days' change of air. Her friends' flat was big enough, she said. We could all do our own thing.

Life flashed into Romi's green, almost lashless eyes. A peculiar shine, like a switch being flicked. From standby to power-on in a split second. 'Yeah, I'd be up for that,' she said. She'd have to discuss it with Phil. But those dates should be fine. Where was Meret going to be?

'With my mother,' Nora said. Turning to me, she asked, 'Is that alright with you? The three of us on the trip?'

I felt it. How important this was to Nora. I hesitated. I didn't much like the idea of endless conversations about children. About what pregnant women were allowed to eat and what they weren't. About how much she was enjoying the anticipation. Underneath, I was already simmering. The trip was going to be a disaster. But all at once, Nora seemed almost to be begging. Something about her was tilting, changing – I was worried. So I pushed all my doubts aside. Just for her. I said, 'As long as we all have our own rooms. Yeah, sure, that's fine.'

Obviously I would have preferred to go with Nora alone. It's so easy when it's just the two of us. Somehow, things fall into place. Romi, on the other hand, is always darting here and there, rushing from one thing to the next. I could tell from the minute we first met. The way she stood there with that pregnant belly. Waiting. Her face always turning to the clock. Although we were on time, Nora and I, and if she hadn't been checking the clock, she would have seen us. Romi wanted nothing more than to be a mother. Instead of completing her master's degree first, establishing a career. Then looking to the future.

Somebody jumps into the water. Slapping waves. The pain intensifies. It's coming from my uterus. Nobody denies the existence of the uterus, but the book next to my deckchair makes no mention of any externally visible signs of female genitalia. No vulva. Only ovaries, fallopian tubes, the uterus, the vagina. Nora would hit the roof if she read it. Once this is over, I should take the book back to the hotel library. A teaching tool. I haven't touched one of those since the teacher in me hung up her chalk. And the minute I did, the last scrap of idealism went as well. I don't need it. Not any more. I need machines that work and staff I can rely on!

Romi's different. When it comes to idealism. I didn't engage much at the time, when she talked about that stuff. About how happy she was with her family, her relationship. I didn't even quote Théophile to see how she'd react. Perhaps I was more restrained because it wasn't the few days before my period, otherwise I wouldn't have been able to hold back. Candour detaching like blood clots. Making space for rage.

Théophile has been saying so for ages: that the primary human right is not to be born into this world. Depression, disease, natural disasters. Violence, injustice, destruction. Or: shame, exhaustion, inequality of opportunity – Nora might put it like that. If she could speak. If she was 'on this side'. But she will be soon. Sooner than her mother might like. Than Romi might like. Romi, who has clearly never stopped to think about what havoc mothers wreak. Without even realising.

Romi doesn't seem to have the first clue who Nora might be. Besides the ever-available friend. The dynamo. The party animal. This isn't the first time, though, that she's lain down and stopped speaking. It's just been a while. Still, Nora always bounces back. She is one of those wobble-bottomed toys that always rights itself. What she needs now is time. A few hours to herself. I'll drop by afterwards. By then things will be sorted at the laundry, too.

A young woman shoots out of the water. Grabs hold of the edge of the pool. Puckers her lips. Sprays a mouthful of water straight into a man's face. Laughs. I can't cope with this today. This noise.

'Excuse me, is there anybody sitting here?'

The sound of wet flip-flops on tile. The face of an older man, friendly, turned to mine. As though we know each other. He's pointing at the deckchair next to mine. I shake my head. I should get up, go back to my room. Rest until Romi arrives.

Romi

NOTE

How late I am, in minutes: seventy-three.
Number of googly-eyed couples in my train carriage: three.
Number of pages I read from that long-form interview with Susan Sontag: three.
(For example: 'Most everything I do seems to have as much to do with intuition as with reason.')
Texts from Dennis: six.
Texts from Szibilla: one.
Texts from Nora: zero.
Texts from Phil: zero.
Checked emails: five times.
What's new: nothing.

The task at hand: draw the blackout curtain. The fabric is stiff and immobile in my hand – it feels as if it's coated in wax – but then it jerks across, top to bottom, swinging defiantly. The room is dark now. I lie down on the neatly made bed. The nausea is worsening, there's a pressure in my throat; I can't settle. Picking myself up, I pull the curtain aside again, and dust glints in the air. I open the window. That's better. My eyes go to the road outside the building. If you follow it, a little further up, around the side of the hotel, you reach a car park: full except for a single space. Opposite my window, on the other side of the road, is a large farm that appears deserted. I hear hammering, then abruptly it stops. A wooden cut-out of a farmer has been stuck into a flowerbed in the verge. Its thick, overlarge finger points at the words on the sign next to it: Farm shop. Self-service. A couple on the pavement are walking uphill. His arm is wrapped around her waist; she walks beside him with dancing steps, briefly touching his bottom every few metres as though by accident: the couple from earlier, at reception. One man, one woman, perhaps an embryo in her belly, who knows.

I'm hit by an unpleasant smell, an invisible cloud forcing its way into the small room. I close the window, the sash hitting the frame with a dull thud. I retch. Sliding down onto the green carpet with the little yellow dots, I lean my back against the wall and reach for my notebook. I breathe deeply in and out, the way the midwife told me; if only it wasn't so stuffy in this room, maybe then I could relax.

'As of today we're fully booked,' the young receptionist had said, fiddling with the neckline of her uniform, a copy of traditional Swiss garb. 'You're lucky we still had rooms available for you and your friend. People like to treat themselves, especially around the bank holiday.'

Turning her attention back to the screen, she went on: 'Ms Szibilla Jakab was allocated the larger room. But I'm sure you'll be happy with the smaller one. It's all ready for you now. We were able to check Ms Jakab in early too.'

She gave me four credit-card-sized drinks vouchers with a smile, black lettering on a gold background; she winked at me as she handed over the key.

I shouldered my rucksack.

As soon as one came available, she said, I could move into a comfort room with a view of the valley, Monday afternoon at the latest – and if I was hungry, the lunch buffet was open, I could get a good meal at a good price.

I tap Szibilla's number. It rings out of sync with the second hand ticking in the clock above the door of my room. Before I go to voicemail, I press the red icon and hang up. Eleven fifty-seven. I place the phone on the floor next to the Susan Sontag book. Szibilla's probably enjoying the view from her more luxurious suite. Or she's already in the dining room, peeling prawns. Phil would hate it, this decadence. It's his lunch break. He'll have found a sunny spot on one of the benches – paving slabs beneath his feet, the University of Applied Sciences behind him – and be studying one of his hobby books, as he calls them: *A Better World: Is Capitalism Played Out?*

I shove the complimentary boiled sweet into my mouth. The Mäder family and the whole team at the Beech Hotel are delighted to welcome me, announces the card on the knee-high table between the bed and the window. Any moment now I'll head off to visit Nora. We will put our heads together, and at long last we will find solutions: to her problems, to mine. Only one more minute.

NOTE

Number of minutes on the phone with Nora's mother yesterday: not quite three. Her voice: soft, cautious; as we talked, I kept picturing a cloth over a just-sharpened knife, and I sensed that at any moment the cloth would tear, the blade be exposed. The mother's name: Annegret. (Goes by Anni.)

She emphasised how important it was for Nora to rest, to sleep, to get her strength back.

Number of seconds I considered going to Berlin anyway, by myself: ten.

Number of words I addressed to Anni the second time I got her answering machine: too many. That we would set off, Szibilla and I, the following day. That I hoped we wouldn't be too much in her hair. That I believed it was really important that we come. Etc.

Number of times I've met up with Nora in the last 102 days: five. The longest of those meetings, six weeks ago. Three of us, including Szibilla. What Nora wanted: first we go to the cinema, then to Buena Onda. But she was different from normal, she seemed nervous all afternoon.

Just before we went our separate ways, the two of us went to the toilet. Nora suddenly so calm. She grabbed my wrist, gazed at me without expression. I hugged her to break the tension, and she said into my ear: 'I envy you. You know that?'

Again I dial Szibilla's number. It goes to voicemail. I put the phone on the table. I have to go: I have to see Nora.

Szibilla

He's already on his way. Says the Miele tech. Rüttimann. He'll be arriving any minute to take a look at the faulty machine. Probably an easy fix.

I hang up. Put the phone next to my laptop. Two clicks. The image fills the screen. A weighing scale, and on it pieces of carved flesh. Fresh from the butcher's, or so you'd think, if it wasn't for the green operating table in the picture. And the HOHL uterine manipulator. Elongated, with traces of blood on it. Underneath, it says: The uterus with the fibroids weighs 323 grams, five times more than normal.

The kettle whines. I reach for it. The water pours sputtering into the porcelain cup, which looks like something from my grandmother's day. It sets the freeze-dried crumbs of coffee swirling, combining into a brown steaming brew. I've already burned my tongue. The laptop is whirring so loudly you'd think it was about to explode. I'll call Romi back later. Once the painkillers have had time to work.

Suddenly it had arrived. The bleeding. A bit too early. The dark-red fleck on the white bathrobe, just now. A towel quickly wrapped around my hips. I rummaged through the basket of amenities in the toilet, looking for a tampon. Then I crumpled the bathrobe into a ball. Getting rid of this symbol of my ability to reproduce. On the way to the toilet, I stuffed it into the container for used towels, my belly throbbing with pain. Such a concrete reminder, the same every month. Of what it means to be human.

To have my uterus removed. No fuss. Like in the seventies. Escaping from this great pain. From the swallowing of painkillers. From this humiliation that lingers.

I would be lying on a sky-blue examination couch in a paper gown, only my vulva exposed. The doctor wouldn't have that dissecting look about him. None of that distaste. Nothing of what I associate with doctors. Rather, something obstinate. Insurgent. Like Théophile. 'Take this thing out of me, doctor. And do it fast,' I'd tell him. Then I'd let him get to work. Moments later, there it would be before me, on the operating table: my uterus. Not just its contents, like before, but the whole of it. And in my belly there would be serenity. Total, this time.

I'd shown Nora the picture. The fibroids in chunks. After she'd handed me the menstrual cup. Less waste, and you don't have to change it as frequently, she said. That was four weeks ago. I'd soon put the cup aside. Told her what I was planning. An endometrial ablation, because they couldn't justify a hysterectomy. My symptoms weren't bad enough. And Nora said it more clearly than ever: 'I think I get it now.' And she went on to say she might get one too, before she got pregnant.

It doesn't stop you getting pregnant, unfortunately, I replied.

But she'd already put some music on. Turned the volume up. Begun to sing along. 'Dick in the Air'. Shaking her head to and fro. She'd looked so casual. That's Nora. In certain situations you just can't be sure how much weight to put on what she says.

I'll try the menstrual cup tomorrow. But now: instant coffee, drinkable at last. Temperature-wise, at least. I'll have to make another foray to the dining room. Order a coffee from the espresso machine. The others will be back as well, I bet. The retired couple who wolfed down heaps of mashed potato and veal. The lone woman. Strikingly upright. Nervous gestures. At the table beneath the Botticelli. *The Birth of Venus.* The young couple. Giving each other cloudy, loved-up looks. Those foolish children of Swiss affluence. I'll flick through the newspaper. Call Romi back. Call the laundry for an update. Then, finally, I'll relax.

I put on my shorts. The white shirt.

Then I go downstairs.

Romi

Through reception. There she is again: the girl in traditional Swiss dress. As I step through the automatic sliding door, I meet the stoic gaze of the two-dimensional farmer across the road. I hurry off uphill. In the distance are the mountains, and at their feet the Rhine, wider than in my memory. Is Szibilla already at Nora's? Unreachable, unlocatable Ms Jakab. I'm walking much too fast, again, as though rushing in the direction of something, but what? I pause, take a deep breath, turn around.

There it is, the Beech Hotel. There's something timeless about the building, as though the upper storeys, clad in dark wood, have always been part of the landscape. The two slopes of the roof meet in a gentle peak, and below that are the balconies belonging to the more expensive rooms. The lower levels, including the extension, are covered almost entirely in a modern glass facade, and at the front is the whirlpool, available at an additional cost and probably not in use today. Has Nora ever been in it? I walk on. Buchenstraße, number 122 – that's where she grew up, and where her mother still lives. Street View yesterday revealed to me a beige-shingled house, brown shutters, a hedge partitioning garden from road. A world penned in. Or 'really fucking cramped', as Nora had once put it.

The road begins to bend, this must be it. I pass through the garden gate, see steps leading to an open porch, a name handwritten next to the bell: Brugger. I push it, wait, hear nothing. To the left of the front door is a knee-high plant pot in the shape of two swans, beaks touching; their long necks form a heart, and in the middle of the heart there are primroses in bloom.

Suddenly the door flies open. A woman stands in the doorway. This must be Anni. She's no higher than my chin. I find myself looking directly at her black hair, at a parting with a glint of grey. She takes a step back. Slender as Nora, with the same long, slightly uptilted nose, the close-set eyes that survey me now, surprised and also stern, as though I hadn't said I was coming.

'Hi,' I say. 'I'm Romi. We spoke on the phone.'

For a moment her expression grows even more forbidding, then slowly it widens, although not by much. The sternness remains. She puts on the trace of a smile, holds out her hand.

'Ah, Romi,' she says in a throaty voice. 'So. You came.'

The smile is not of a piece with the rest of her.

'Did you – perhaps you didn't get my message? I didn't want to disturb you too late in the evening.'

'Yes, yes,' she says casually, stroking her tunic, a coral-coloured floral design presumably from Boutique Chic, where Nora tries to maintain some semblance of order (as she puts it) while women over sixty ransack shelves and hangers, seeking something to make them young again and examining textiles as though they were precious years that could be restored by reaching for their purses. 'My mother? She's one of a kind, that old bag,' Nora has always said. She must be in her late sixties now, and she looks it, despite the thick rind of make-up and the youthful clothing. 'It's nice to finally meet you,' I say, 'albeit under less than pleasant circumstances.' But Anni has already turned away. She is pointing at the spiral staircase, saying she assumes I'll want to go straight up. We ascend together, me behind her; Anni moves at my pace.

'You really didn't have to come,' she says, climbing the steps. 'Nothing's happened yet.'

'So what's wrong with Nora, exactly?' I ask. 'Summer cold?'

'No,' says Anni. 'I don't think so.'

'So what is it then?'

Anni, reaching the top of the stairs, turns to look at me. 'Well,' she says, and her expression is just the same as before, somehow switched off, so peculiarly detached. Nora showed up out of the blue the day before yesterday, she tells me, one day earlier than expected, with Meret on her back. She unfastened the baby and collapsed into her childhood bed. Then she'd said one thing, and one thing only: that she couldn't go to Berlin after all, and that she, Anni, was to let me and Szibilla know. Now, Nora is responding to no one, even Meret, although this is probably also due to the sedative she's taken, which hopefully will do her good. She, Anni, is glad that Nora has come, because at her mother's house she will recover more quickly, and this way Meret can be taken care of too.

As if on cue, I hear a child crying downstairs, and before I can ask any more questions, Anni rushes past me down the steps. I'm not to bother Nora for too long, she says, and: she'll make me a cup of tea, since I'm here.

I'm alone now, outside a bedroom door affixed with four letters in different shades of pastel: N, O, R, A. I step inside. The door squeaks. One of the shutters is closed, and the panelled walls make the room seem even darker.

Nora is lying on her side on a single mattress in the middle of the room. Her legs are bent her kneecaps like two stones, one on top of the other beneath the thin cotton blanket. Her red hair is faded. I take a couple of steps towards her, bend down. Her eyes are closed and her skin appears transparent, a shimmer of tiny veins beneath. I place one hand on her cool forehead, the other on her upper back.

'Nora, hey, it's me,' I say. 'What's going on? How are you feeling?'

No reaction.

'Nora, hello? Can you hear me?'

Nothing.

'Can you tell me what's wrong?'

Nora is lying as still as a mannequin, and she herself is elsewhere, some place far away: I feel paralysed. For a moment, I hover. Then I sit down on the floor beside the mattress.

'Is there anything I can do for you? Do you want something to drink?'

Nora doesn't respond. Her pulse is slow and even. I stroke her back. Her hair smells of hay. Is she asleep?

NOTE

Number of doors in Nora's room: one.
Number of windows: two.
I draw a circle with an imaginary piece of string: the distance from Nora's body to the four walls is exactly the same.
Number of wishes: one. Lie down next to her, feel her back against my stomach, dive down to where she is, slumber, together, then wake up at the same time and talk, wildly and without restraint.

It's so quiet in this room, as though we're in a box that muffles everything. Sounds, but colours too. The walls are unfinished wood, they are marked, encoded; these are the walls Nora used to wish were white. As a child, she told me once, she had seen lizards and snakes in the natural patterns of the wood, figures that transformed over the years, morphing into sprites and fairies, into evil witches, into murderers from horror films, into paternal shoulders, turned and cold, into Baubo and the other mythological figures which have always interested her. The latter are the only ones she took with her, in spirit, when she left this room.

Three years ago, during her first major crisis with Emrik, she was seized with the desire to clear out her room, to throw out all the old things or take them away – to be able, at last, to truly leave. She hadn't managed it, as she chipperly informed me later, at least not entirely: she had left her photo albums and diaries at her mother's, in this house which smelled perpetually of lunch, of washing powder and woollen slippers, of heavy carpets and the things hidden beneath. She didn't know where else to keep mementos from her childhood and her teenage years, she didn't have room for them at her place, so where else? But really, she said, none of that stuff mattered.

The office chair is on wheels, the desk is the perfect height, and on it is an empty glass. In the wastepaper basket next to it is a blister pack and nothing else. Two photographs are pinned to the wall above the desk.

NOTE

Estimated size of the room: eighteen square metres.
Number of years Nora lived here: just under seventeen.
Format of the photographs above the desk: A4.
Number of years that have passed since they were taken: many.

1) *Nora at about twelve years old, in a neon-yellow swimsuit, standing on a riverbank, head bowed, eyes on the water; beside her is a man of fifty or so, one hand on her shoulder, the other resting on his soft waist, a cigarette in the corner of his mouth; on the man's bare, hairy stomach, a word is written in black permanent marker: pussy.*

2) *Nora as a toddler with a dummy and a pink hairband; on it, scrawled in the same marker, are the words: up yours.*

Nora hasn't moved an inch.

'Did you do that? The photos, I mean?' I ask.

Nora lies very still.

'I'd really like to talk to you about all this, about family and your memories and everything.'

The two pictures are the only personal elements in the room. The rest is interchangeable, at least on the surface: the desk, the colourful polka-dotted curtain, the three cardboard boxes in the corner. How long has it been since Nora was last here?

I kneel next to Nora, asking, 'Are your diaries in there? The photos?'

Nora's thin lips are chapped, they are tightly closed. You couldn't get a piece of paper in between them. I feel like shaking her. I slip the nail of my index finger into the soft bed of my thumbnail instead, breaking the skin.

'I can't believe you're just lying there not saying anything! Nora? Give me some kind of a sign! Please!'

I sit back down at the desk. Only now do I see his resemblance to Nora, the man in the photograph, that grin; it's him, then, the father who disappeared when she was fourteen, who made an explicit decision to walk out, unlike my dad. A dark red stripe gapes open on my thumb, beside the nail, a centimetre long. There's something missing, just a shred of skin. Where's the pencil?

NOTE

Number of things happening at the same time: …
Number of options Nora had, places she could have gone, instead of coming to her mother's: plenty.
Number of trains I would have preferred to take today: three. One to Munich, then a change to Nuremberg, and from Nuremberg to Berlin.
Number of trains I took: one. No changes.

One train comes in and another train leaves; one is travelling to Berlin and the other to the Rhine Valley; one took a seventeen-year-old Nora to the city, the other seems to have remained in her childhood bedroom; one has always been the master of her decisions, and the repudiation of them; the other is here, refusing to be moved, quiet as never before: Nora is silent. And I want to talk and do nothing but talk and feel and think, but—

'Nora, I can't take much more of this. Please say something!'

The door handle is cold. It has no purpose. I have to go downstairs, find Anni.

Szibilla

'There you are, at last!' says Romi. A hum in the background. Probably a car. 'Where have you been?'

'I haven't moved from the spot,' I say. 'If you can consider the hotel one spot. Anyway, my phone tells me I've called you back about three times in the last hour.'

'True,' says Romi, adding that she's been with Nora, so she put her phone on silent. Now she's on her way back to the hotel. Do I want to grab a coffee?

I look at my restless leg. Sounds good, I say. I tell her I'm already in the dining room, I may as well wait for her here. Although I do have a massage booked. The only appointment they have available today.

From my table, you can see straight into the lobby. People come and go. Madame Ibuprofen has reached my uterus, where she washes back and forth. My leg keeps joggling. And yet. The period pains are nearly gone. For another solid hour or two. And the washing machine is back up and running. Even Rüttimann sounded relieved.

Here she is already, Romi. Hurrying through reception. Glancing at the rack of newspapers and magazines. Faintly harried, as ever. She's thin these days. Generally different-seeming. As though her body has been taken apart and reassembled. All the parts are in their original place, only, a millimetre out of position. Her pregnancy: conspicuous. In that tight-fitting shirt, at least.

Romi slows. Her gaze sweeps across the mostly empty tables, high ponytail swinging back and forth. Now her eyes fall on me: a look almost of surprise.

'There you are!' she says, stopping in front of me. At that moment the waitress arrives with my cappuccino. Romi orders one herself, then gives me a hug. She's stronger than she looks.

'How are you doing?' I ask.

Romi takes the chair across from mine. Picks at her fingernails. The skin around them is already ragged.

She pauses. The creases in her forehead are new. They suit her. Give her a rougher look.

'Honestly, not great,' she says. 'You know Nora has completely stopped talking – hasn't said a word for days! Did you realise that?'

I give a tiny shake of my head. Romi continues. 'It's so weird,' she says. Nora didn't speak at all when she went to see her. She just lay there. In this nearly empty room. Her old childhood bedroom.

'Look, there's no need to worry,' I cut in. 'I'm sure Nora will be better soon.'

Now Romi looks me right in the eye. There are three grains of brown in the left green iris. They look almost dabbed on. I've never noticed them before.

'Nora's unrecognisable!' she says. 'It's literally like she's unconscious!'

The waitress sets down a cup of coffee in front of her. Carries the tray on to the next table, balancing its contents. Romi is still studying me. Unblinking.

'Do you have any idea what's wrong with Nora?' she asks me. Loud voices are drifting in from reception. A couple with a teenage girl in tow. Three fat suitcases on wheels behind a giant of a man. The girl a speck beside him. The woman kneeling in between them, turned towards the man. They're talking over each other.

'Nora is processing something,' I say. 'It's a protective silence. She'll come out of it eventually, and she'll be stronger on the other side.'

The girl's face twists into a smirk. The man's voice breaks off, the bass dropping out. Only the woman is still audible. The Queen of the Night's solo. A classic, this family.

Romi is back to staring out of the window. One hand working on the nails of the other.

'I'd like to know what she's withdrawing from,' Romi says. She mumbles something about how Anni isn't exactly pleased to see us, and that she's being very tight-lipped. Then she goes on, more clearly: 'When I came back down from Nora's room, Anni was already waiting for me with a cup of tea. She made it very clear she had to rush straight out, said she had shopping to do. Meret seemed very shy, but maybe she was just sleepy, who knows. Anni didn't want me to babysit while she went out, although I thought it might do some good if the two of us went back upstairs! When I asked if it might be best to get some help, a doctor or something, Anni just shook her head. She said she wanted to wait, at least until tomorrow.'

'Well, on that point I agree with Anni,' I said. 'We shouldn't jump the gun.'

Snap. Romi's face swivels back towards mine.

'Something terrible must have happened!' she says. 'And I have no idea what.'

Each word is louder than the last. More rapid-fire.

'Slow down, Romi,' I say. 'Just listen, okay? There's a lot you don't know, alright. Nora hasn't been doing well for months. It's not just since yesterday!'

Romi hesitates. She seems to be considering this. Then, more calmly, she says, 'She's been dealing with a lot lately, you're right.'

I take three big gulps of my cappuccino. The temperature's ideal. I put the cup back. Say slowly, 'Moving out of Emrik's place was by far the best decision Nora has made in the last three years.'

'Yeah, maybe,' Romi says. The furrows in her brow are back. 'But then, what's got her into this state now?'

Slowly but surely, I feel the pain come knocking again. Deep down. It can't be – not yet, not this soon.

'Oh, it'll be some straw that broke the camel's back,' I say. 'She's often come to my place when she felt that way in the past. When she realised one of the courses she was taking wasn't for her after all. When the loneliness got too much for her. After a fight with Emrik. Or because of the pregnancy. She'd just lie down. Wouldn't speak. Mostly she just wanted to know someone was there. Somebody to give her a little nudge. Show her that life goes on. Has to go on. But not too soon. And not in a demanding way. She always got back up again, and always when I least expected it.'

'You've seen her like this before?'

I nod. 'This time the downswing is a bit more pronounced, I guess. She's processing certain things. Becoming more independent. But like I said. Soon she'll be the old Nora again. And, Romi, if you make a big song and dance of it now, you won't be doing her any favours. Okay? The opposite, actually. Anyway, tell me. How are things with you?'

Romi is eyeing me with scepticism. She scratches her temple. 'I'm feeling pretty frazzled, to be honest.'

'Overworked? Then we've come to the right place. Have you been to the pool yet?'

Romi seems surprised. Says: 'Not job-wise, that's for sure. Overworked, I mean.' After a brief pause, she goes on: 'I'm barely getting any work at all. And no, I haven't been to the pool. Does it cost extra?'

'You're still with the publishing house?'

'No, not any more,' she says. She doesn't really want to talk about it, I can see it in her face. Still, she goes on, telling me she's holding out for a permanent position. They've been dangling the prospect of one at the publisher's where she did her internship, and until then they're throwing her odd jobs here and there. But unless things pick up soon, she'll have to fall back on speech-to-text reporting.

'So you're dependent on Phil's income?' I ask. 'Does it pay well enough for that, being an adjunct at the university?'

'Yeah, we're mainly living off his salary at the moment. Hopefully not for much longer, though.'

'And if he walks out and stops paying for everything, what then?'

'I have a degree, and we live in Switzerland. I'll be fine.' Romi is staring past me, through the window. She says, 'This is where Nora grew up. What do you think – why does Anni want to keep us at arm's length?'

Back to the topic at hand. No surprise there.

'She'll have her reasons,' I say. 'Do you know she used to work at this hotel? She only left a few years ago.'

Romi shakes her head. 'Right now I don't feel like I know

anything at all. Everything seems so disjointed. I can only see what's right in front of my nose, and even then only barely. It's like all the connections between things have been severed.'

She swallows. Then she continues: 'I haven't been there for Nora over the past few weeks, not properly, and I really am sorry about that. Time's just been flying, and there was so much to discuss with Phil and Dennis. Not to mention that Leon's been much clingier than usual.'

'Dennis?' I ask. 'The guy who was with you at the supermarket the other day? The one you told us about?'

'Yeah. We've been together since the end of February. It's kind of a crazy story.'

She gives a quick smile and pushes the cappuccino away. 'I'm nauseous all the time now. Probably why I'm feeling so strange. Morning sickness. It's a nightmare.'

'Is it his kid? Dennis's?'

'Phil is the father, there's no doubt about that.'

'And is he okay with it? You having this fling?'

Romi looks up. 'It's a relationship,' she says firmly. 'And yes, Phil gave his consent from the get-go. They've even met, actually, him and Dennis. Although that doesn't mean it isn't painful for Phil, of course, or that it'll be easy to live like this.'

'You see this as something long-term?'

'Absolutely! Is it still fresh? Yes, but what Dennis and I have is very special, it's …' She's grasping for words, and I'm thinking how desperately I want to stand up. To fetch another painkiller from upstairs.

'So how exactly are you planning for this to work?' I ask instead. 'Two men, two children. That's a recipe for chaos!'

'You don't find the right balance for these things overnight,' Romi says. 'It's a process. It takes a lot of communication, a lot of cooperation.'

'You don't think it would make more sense to be alone?'

A long moment passes. Then Romi says, 'You know, it's amazing really. We've been sitting here for fifteen minutes and you sound like you've got my whole life figured out. And Nora's. I've often wondered where you get that from, this total certainty about everything and everyone.'

'We've known each other for more than fifteen minutes, Romi.'

'Known each other?' She leans back in her chair. Studies the Botticelli on the wall opposite. Fleet-footed Venus with the wind in her hair.

'Can I give you a piece of advice?' I ask. 'Just from an outside perspective, speaking as a harmless idiot who knows nothing about relationships?'

Now Romi can't help but laugh, although her face immediately resumes its earnest expression.

'Don't you think it's about time you took a long hard look at your relationship with freedom?' I ask. 'I'm thinking of Phil here, too, and his freedom. Because – and I'm just asking – do you really believe that people choose this kind of set-up of their own free will?'

'Hard to imagine, I know, but you're not the only person who's been giving this some thought,' Romi says promptly. Less annoyed than I'd expected, more weary. 'Obviously that's been on my mind, and not just in relation to me and Phil.'

'What, then?'

Romi crosses her arms over her belly. 'Lately I keep thinking about my parents. Their lives, their inadequacies. My father's affair, for instance. The way he dealt with that, and how it affected his reaction to my new relationship.'

'When was it?' I ask. 'The affair?'

'Years ago,' Romi replies. 'My mother found out, and in the end he had to choose: affair or family. He stayed with us – well, I'm sure you can imagine. Long story short, it didn't work out well for him, or for any of us. But why am I telling you this?'

'I'm a big proponent of clear decision-making,' I say. 'Surely you know me well enough to realise that, at least.'

'But you don't know my family,' Romi says. 'And you certainly don't know my dad.'

I wait for a moment. Then I ask, 'Did he tell you so himself? That it didn't work out for him?'

Romi shrugs. 'Touchy subject.'

That's all I get out of her. I glance at the clock. 'I need to go. Time for my massage.'

'You haven't been to see Nora yet, have you?' Romi asks.

I get to my feet. 'I'll go this afternoon. Any earlier would be jumping the gun. By then she may be ready to have dinner with us.'

'I find that hard to imagine.'

Romi is still fiddling with her nails, picking away at the skin around them.

'See you at reception, half past five?' I ask.

Romi glances up. 'Fine,' she says.

Romi

I shouldn't have: I shouldn't have left the window open. Although the stench isn't just coming from outside, it's elsewhere too – but where? Planting both hands on the soft mattress, I let myself slip sideways onto the bed. My neck is tense. I could take another nap. I'd love to know where Szibilla's aggression comes from. She may be right about one thing, though: we should keep a cool head for now, as best we can, and have some faith in Nora. My phone vibrates. A text from Dennis, and ten minutes ago I got one from Phil as well. Dennis is asking if I got in alright, Phil where Leon's sun hat is. Dennis sends me lots of kisses, Phil a hug, and suddenly I'm hearing my father's voice, harsh: 'You don't see happiness when it's right in front of your face.'

There's a rumble in my stomach. Something is pressing its way up my gullet, and I stumble into the bathroom. The dark jet hits the centre of the bowl. Rinse once, wipe mouth. I shouldn't have bothered with the coffee.

I walk gingerly back into the bedroom, take my notebook out of my bag.

NOTE

Number of nights I will be sleeping here: four.
Of those nights, how many alone: most likely four.
Number of times I have told my father about my new relationship: one.
Number of words he used in reply: twelve. (You – don't – see – happiness –)
My room number: 301.

My room number then: 217.
Number of days that passed before I told Phil about Dennis: one.

His body tense beside me on the sofa. His hand slowly slipping off my leg. His silence. Cough. Who was he, this Dennis guy, and how long had I known him?

'Since yesterday.'

What did it mean, he asked, for him and for us?

'I don't know that either.'

Did I still want to be with him, Phil asked.

And I answered without hesitation: 'Yes.'

He got up heavily and went into the kitchen, arms swinging back and forth as always, gait erect, the shadow on his neck and the contours of his chin all the more sharply drawn, the angle of his jaw so immediately distinctive, the place I loved to kiss. And I didn't know yet that a bundle of cells was already nesting in my uterine lining, ready to grow, another bond between myself and Phil. I did not yet know the tremendous variability of the word 'us'.

NOTE

Number of options left to Phil (in other words, Phil's freedom):

1. *Say no*
2. *Give me an ultimatum: either/or*
3. *Walk out*
4. *Stay*
5. *...*

I reach for the phone, text Dennis the three numbers in three separate messages: *2. 1. 7.* I get under the covers. There is a beam of light cast across them, and I trace its contours, around and around. My belly is heavy, growing ever more rounded. I am immensely hungry yet my appetite is small. We lay together in our room, the first one, Dennis and I.

NOTE

A slice of cake on the lips. I touch the velvety glaze with my tongue, wait for it to melt, then take a bite. Taste of chocolate in my mouth. Beside me is a baby, small and fragile, its skin still translucent, shot through with veins that seem to run haphazardly from nape of neck to coccyx, from flank to stomach, from navel to groin, from thigh to foot: the baby is motionless. Too small for this world. I nestle the child to my breast – he sucks and smacks his lips; he melts and dwindles and passes, like time. Something is always too soon, too late, too greatly wanted, too little loved, too egotistically conceived, too fickle, too fluid, too fast. Myself, alone with the seven; the seven that cuts into my tongue. I uncover myself. A blanket slips to the floor; it is already morning. Light on the wallpaper before me, wandering. Someone is coming towards me: head, trunk, legs, in perpetual motion. I reach out, grab something warm; the second hand ticks.

Eyes shut.

Eyes open, 4.09 p.m. A text from Dennis, *Wish you were here.* Eyes shut. I toss and turn. Such desire as I lie here, desire for his breath on my cheek, for the sound of his voice, for his tongue on my breast. I see a back, see shoulders, a strong solid neck, and I put my hands on this neck, move them slowly upwards, millimetre by millimetre, through his hair until I reach his temples, clasp his head, turn his face to mine, and I glide on top of him, spread myself.

'Is it just about the sex?' Phil asked, 102 days ago, re-emerging from the kitchen.

'No,' I said.

'So what is it then? What is it you want from this guy?' he went on, and after a brief pause, 'What is it that I can't give you?'

'We promised we'd be honest with each other, you and I, and I am. There's something about him that attracts me, and I'd like to find out what that is. If that's okay with you.'

'You don't belong to me.'

'What does that mean?'

'You don't belong to me any more than anything else on this planet belongs to me, I know that, Romi. But it still hurts like hell.'

'I don't want to hurt you. I never wanted that!'

'I don't know how I'm going to respond to this,' Phil says.

'I understand.'

'We'll have to find out.'

'Yes.'

'It will take time.'

'Yes.'

Eyes open. Everything is still here. Eighteen square metres, a stifling hole. My shirt drenched in sweat. Five twenty-six. A quick cold shower, two blasts of deodorant under my arms, some kohl around the eyes, slip into my dress, into my sandals. Notebook, phone and wallet in my bag. Szibilla will already be waiting. Perhaps we'll get along, the two of us. For Nora's sake.

Phil

She could at least have cleared the breakfast table. It's all still there, the yoghurt, the spoon mired in the honey, the open bag of muesli, her coffee half drunk. As always, she was leaving in a hurry and forgot the rest. My phone vibrates: The sun hat must be in with the rest of his clothes somewhere.

In front of me is a pile of scarves and slightly grubby T-shirts. One with Spiderman on it, one with the inscription *Little Adventurer*, a thin pullover made of some ribbed fabric with navy sleeves. Here is Romi's scarf from London, a gift from me, many years ago. There it is, the sun hat, emblazoned with two grinning dogs. Leon is already sitting on the stairs in the hall.

'Can we get an ice cream too?' he asks.

'We can,' I say, 'but you can't have it until tomorrow.'

'Is there ice cream where Mama is too?'

'Yeah, of course.'

'How many sleeps until she's back?'

'Four. See, as many sleeps as you've got fingers.'

'Is she sleeping in a big bed?'

'I think probably, yeah. A nice big hotel bed.'

'Maybe she's dreaming about us. About us having ice cream together. The three of us!'

'Who knows.'

As if I didn't have enough to do. Nine days – no, eight – to finish the paper. Leon is already out the door. Again, I'm picturing it. Romi and Dennis in bed, face to face. She puts her arm around him and pulls him in close. The way she always does, with that smile, the dimples left and right. It gets her anything. I'd rather not know if she ended up in bed with Dennis on the first night. I turn the key in the lock. Feel a pressure against the sole of my foot. I shake out my shoe: a pebble.

Down the steps, open the letterbox. Inside there's a flyer urging me to vote Liberal in the next elections, a fashion catalogue, three envelopes. Two are plain and white, one pink. Our address is lettered in gold. I open it. *Made with Love!* it announces on the front, bold violet script across a photograph in black and white. It's of a half-naked baby, eyes closed. I turn over the card. On the back it reads: *On 16 May we were lucky enough to welcome our Antonela Filipa in our arms. We are infinitely happy and grateful. Dani, Simone and Rhea.*

I slide the card back into the envelope and open the second. A statement from the bank. The third: the annual financial records for www.romischreibt.ch. A website for female authors, Romi's idea. Has it always been registered under my name?

Vinzenz comes around the corner. 'Hey, Phil!' He stops as he draws level. 'Picking out something nice?'

Nodding in the direction of the catalogue, he places a bottle of suntan lotion on the letterbox.

'"Bonprix". Doesn't sound very promising,' I say.

He nods. 'By the way, I'm throwing a little garden party tomorrow and I'd like to use the fire pit. Is that okay with you? You're all very welcome to come, needless to say!'

'That's kind of you. I'll let you know, alright? Although Romi definitely can't make it.'

'Well, then that's one less person to consult!'

I push the two white envelopes back into the letterbox. We walk outside through the main door. 'I've been meaning to ask you for ages,' I say, 'that round table upstairs, is that yours?'

Vinzenz thinks for a moment. 'You mean the one next to the stairs? Isn't that your grandmother's?'

'Not that I'm aware,' I say. 'I'll ask the Hubers. We could find a use for it.'

Vinzenz shoves his hands into the pockets of his trousers and leans against the doorframe.

'You can always send Leon up to our place,' he says. 'While Romi's away.'

'That's nice of you,' I say. 'And likewise, Clara and Sebastian are always welcome at ours.'

'When is Romi back?'

'Wednesday. Are the kids with you until tomorrow or the day after?'

Vinzenz takes a pouch of tobacco out of his pocket and starts to roll a cigarette.

'Monday night,' he says, and licks the rolling paper. Then he sparks up and takes a long drag.

'How are things with Marie, anyway?' I ask.

Slowly, Vinzenz exhales smoke. 'Don't ask,' he says, taking another drag. 'But let me tell you, I never thought in a million years we'd crash and burn like this. She wants everything now. Including sole custody.'

'That's rough,' I say. 'I'm sure she won't get away with that.'

'Yeah, but just the fact that she thinks – she thinks she can take everything!' he says.

I wait for a moment. Then I ask, 'Do you want to have a chat about it tonight? After the kids have gone to bed?'

Vinzenz takes another pull of his cigarette before stubbing it out half-smoked on the ground. Then, without answering, he flicks it into the bin next to the main door.

'Have you seen Leon?' I ask.

'He's just around the corner with Clara and Sebi, telling feminist jokes.' Vinzenz guffaws, but stops when he sees I'm not laughing with him. I take my leave and start walking towards my bike. He calls after me, 'By the way, about the day after tomorrow. I've got a couple of old friends coming round, nothing big. Drop by, why don't you? As for tonight, let's play it by ear, alright?'

'Alright!'

I'm still clutching the pink envelope in my left hand. Dani and Simone. Haven't seen them for ages. I put the envelope in the trailer, attach the trailer to the bike, climb on.

She wants everything. I used to think we did. Have everything, that is. When Romi lay naked in the muted light of the birthing room. Leon at her breast, still so tiny. When she murmured, 'This is it, this is it.' Her beautiful dark hair. Sopping wet. If only it were that simple, this 'everything'.

Who knows what will happen once Romi figures out what's going on with her. Perhaps this thing with Dennis will fall apart?

'Dad?'

'Leon? Are you coming?'

'Can I sit in the trailer?'

'Sure.'

'Are we buying chocolate ice cream or strawberry ice cream?'

'Both.'
'We're getting a tub each?'
'Just this once, but yes.'

Szibilla

There she is, Romi. All dolled up, like she's got something to hide. Still, it suits her, the shadowy quality to her face. She bounces down the stairs in her red dress. Hesitates. Places her key on the reception desk

'Shall we?' Romi asks. She adds, 'You look more relaxed.'

She's right. It's Malita Sousa's doing. The hotel's massage therapist, in whose capable hands I have spent a full hour and a half. The second painkiller did the rest.

We step through the door. I push my sunglasses off my forehead onto my nose. We are following the street, moving downhill. Romi clears her throat several times. Must be ill at ease with silence.

'Apparently they're going to be rewilding the Rhine,' she begins eventually. 'But you've probably heard about that already.'

'Yeah. The new flood defence project. Honestly, it sounds about right for Switzerland. Building these new dams, putting concrete limits on things. Straightening the course of the river. The smooth handling of it all.'

'Handling?' Romi repeats. 'Sounds like you're talking about your rental car.'

When I don't react, she carries on: 'The current dams are way too old. If they break, everything around here will be flooded. And surely you're interested in the idea of making more space for nature?'

'This project is mostly bullshit,' I say. 'They've only planned for three stepping-stone biotopes – for twenty-six kilometres of river! And not a single area of quality wetland. They should do it properly or not at all.'

Romi puts her hand on my shoulder. Asks, 'Is everything okay?'

An unpleasant warmth where her hand is resting. I step aside. Romi pulls her hand back.

'Yes,' I say. 'Whatever that means.'

'Do you think we can do it? Rally round, I mean, for Nora?' Romi asks.

'How do you mean?'

'Be there for her, together.'

'I think we have rather different ideas about that.'

Romi glances at me sidelong. 'What do you mean?'

'Didn't we just talk about this?' I ask in reply.

Three motorbikes drive past us. Roaring machines. Now the house, on the left.

'Here we are,' I say.

We cross the twee little garden. Romi asks no more questions. Up the steps. She presses the bell. Instantly Anni is standing in front of us, as though she's been waiting on the other side of the door. She greets us with that smile I know. Anything but genuine. She doesn't want either of us here. But she meets Romi's eye. Shakes her hand noticeably longer. She's met me before too, three years ago. On that occasion, Nora told me on the journey down to just let her mother talk. Push back as little as possible. And she added, 'There's not really any other way to deal with my mum.'

Nora had seemed very different. Mostly, over dinner with her permanently sweet-and-sour-smiling mum, she kept silent. Anni probably thought we were a couple. Once I realised that, I patted

Nora's thigh. I should have left well enough alone, because no sooner were we out of the house than Nora turned and snarled – I'd never heard her speak to me like that before. 'What a stupid fucking idea,' she said. And something about deliberate provocation. I could pull that shit with anybody else, for all she cared, but not her mother. I told her she shouldn't take her mum so seriously, and Nora gave me a furious look. 'As if it was that easy!' she said. I had no idea what it was like, she told me, growing up with a mother like that. Obvious enough what she meant. But then why come here now? Why not come to me?

Romi and Anni are staring at me. Like I've missed something. I'm in no mood for Anni. To think that Nora once grew in that womb. That she lived in this house. Awful. She deserved better. But childhood is childhood. Genes are genes. What she makes of it now is another matter.

Has Nora said anything since her last visit, Romi wants to know. Anni answers coolly: 'No.' There's nothing to report, she tells us. We can see for ourselves.

At that moment, Meret comes toddling in, tousle-haired. Romi kneels, and the girl immediately lets herself be scooped up. Romi stands. Staggers. She's gone very pale. Her fingers clutch at my arm.

'Romi?' I ask.

'Sorry,' she says. 'My vision went black for a minute there. I'll be fine.'

'Do you want to sit down for a bit?' I ask.

'A glucose tablet, maybe?' Anni asks.

Romi refuses both. Already turning away, she says we should go up and see Nora. Anni stays downstairs. We're standing outside Nora's sometime bedroom. Knock. Nothing. Enter.

Nora is lying on a mattress. Face buried in the covers. Romi hovers in the doorway. I take a few steps towards Nora. Bend down.

'Hey, Nora!' I say. 'We're here! Get up and put on some fresh clothes. We'll wait for you outside.'

Now Romi is next to me. She puts Meret down. Runs a hand through Nora's hair. She says, almost pleadingly, 'Nora. Why don't we go out somewhere? The village, maybe, the Rhine? We could go for a walk. Get a coffee somewhere, something like that. What do you think?'

But there is no response from Nora. She really is still 'on the other side'. Nothing to be done. We'd be better leaving her alone. But Meret is plucking at her mother's hair. I pick her up. She starts to scream. I press her to me and gradually she subsides, her face buried in my shoulder.

'It's too soon,' I tell Romi. And, under my breath, 'We can't get through to Nora like this. We need to let her rest a little longer.'

Romi gets to her feet. Again, she looks unsteady. Grabs me for support. This time only for a moment.

'Have you actually had anything to eat today?' I ask. 'Anything substantial?' Romi stares at me bewildered.

'We'll come back later,' I say, taking hold of her forearm. 'You need something greasy. Potato salad. Käsespätzle. You can't help Nora in a state like this. And you can't carry a child. Jittery body, jittery nerves.'

It's remarkable, but Romi follows.

Anni

First they show up uninvited, and then they go marching straight in. The way that Szibilla struts about the place! Like she's heading into football practice. As far as I'm concerned they could have taken the kid this time, and kept her. But I shouldn't think like that. I'd better pull the blind. Meret is sitting on the kitchen floor. I get the puzzle and the book of baby animals and set them in front of her. I'm hoping she'll play with her toys while I'm on the phone.

I go to the telephone and dial Dorothe's number. It rings. Usually she's free around this time. She can't not pick up, surely. I hang up and go over to the sink. Squirt a bit of soap onto the sponge. The teapot's been needing a good clean for ages. The water foams.

Nora has always been a handful. When she was five years old she used to kick me in the shins whenever she wanted something and didn't get it straight away. Then immediately she'd run off and hide in the strangest places and refuse to talk. But now there's something really wrong. Did she really only take the sedatives, or was there something else? I put the teapot next to the cups to dry. Wipe the last bits of foam off the draining board with a tea towel. Meret is pushing the jigsaw pieces around on the floor. She's already taking after her mother. When she did that little vanishing act earlier, I feared the worst. A tumble down the basement stairs, a front door left ajar. And on my watch, at that! But no, there she was, stock-still in the corner behind the living-room door, face to the wall. It's like she isn't quite all there. I hold the tea towel under the tap, then turn the water off and wring out the cloth.

The telephone rings. Dorothe.

'Were you asleep?' I ask.

'No, no,' she says, 'I was in the basement. How are you?'

'Fine, fine,' I say. 'But I'm afraid I can't come to the Café Schneider this afternoon.'

'I thought you were going to bring Meret?'

'I don't think I'd feel comfortable doing that.'

'I see. Alright, then we'll see each other for the excursion on Tuesday.'

Dust has been collecting in the corner of the living room. I desperately need to hoover.

'Probably not,' I say. 'I'll be looking after the little one for the next couple of days. Didn't I tell you that?'

'Oh yes, that's right! Is Nora already off on holiday, then?'

'She's staying here.'

'Then why isn't she looking after the baby?'

'She needs a break. I'll call you again in a day or two.'

I put the phone down and roll the blind back up. I return to the kitchen. Meret gazes at me wide-eyed. These kids, they're always wanting something.

'Are you hungry?' I ask.

She looks away.

The aluminium foil is wrapped tightly around the cake, and I carefully peel it away. The cake looks good. I cut the slice in two.

'You can have some of that later, okay?'

I put a piece on a plate for Nora, add a glass of water. She didn't touch the hot chocolate I took up earlier. But she'll have to drink something sooner or later. Meret scrambles up the stairs in front of me. At the top she turns and stares, looking at me like I'm some sort of ghost. She can talk, at least a bit. But with me? No, not with me. She turns back to the door. She reaches the handle, barely, and opens the door.

'Mama?' Always that devoted whine.

Mama, Mama, Mama. Nora never came to me like that. She always wanted her dad. Daddy, Daddy, Daddy. And not just after what happened with Flops. You leave the dog in the car one time, and you get nothing but drama. Nora never realised what good care I took of her. But that's about to change. It has to.

Meret holds out a puzzle piece to Nora. It drops onto the pillow. I put Nora's plate next to the mattress and pull Meret away. She'll get her piece downstairs, at the table.

'Nora, look, I've brought you a slice of your favourite cake.'

She's rolled onto her other side since I was last upstairs.

'You know, I had a thought earlier. How would you fancy a nice quiet evening in front of the telly? I was thinking, maybe, once you've eaten something and you're feeling better, we could do that. There's a good film on, a German one, at quarter past eight. We'll make popcorn and watch it, eh?'

Meret is still looking at Nora. Her little hands are resting on her knees.

'Mama wake?'

I shake my head.

'Shh,' I say, ruffling her hair. Then to Nora: 'I'll take good care of Meret. You just try and get your strength back! We'll have plenty of time together after that. Why don't you try a bit of cake? It's always better the day after, you know that. This one tastes amazing.'

I nudge the plate closer to Nora. She must genuinely be asleep.

Romi

The dining room is packed with hotel guests. Some have embraced evening dress, others wear jeans and sweatshirts. Szibilla has the menu in her hands and a glass of prosecco fizzing in front of her – I was only gone a minute, nipping to the loo. She's poured me one as well. I pull the chair back and it bumps across the carpet. The waiter is already there, depositing a bread basket in front of us. I cast a quick glance at the menu and choose the cheapest thing on it, a soup, and a glass of tap water. Szibilla orders the vegetarian main course. The waiter leaves, heading through the large room towards the bar; Szibilla slides the menu underneath the salt shaker and raises her glass of prosecco.

'Cheers!'

I point to my empty water glass.

'You're not going to have even a single tiny sip?' she asks.

I tell her no and take a piece of bread.

'May I?'

She waits for my nod, then reaches for my prosecco and drinks, runs her tongue over her lips and asks, 'You're taking the no alcohol thing pretty seriously, aren't you?'

'I've lost my taste for it these days anyway, so it's quite practical. I've been drinking more apple juice instead. No more hangovers.'

'Shall I order you one?' Szibilla asks. 'My treat, obviously. Don't want you keeling over again.'

I decline with a wave of my hand. There's no need, I say, the

57

three glucose tablets I've just taken will do the trick. Szibilla takes another sip from her glass, surveying me.

'I don't know much about having a baby,' she says at last, 'but it seems logical that people put on weight. So how is it you've lost some, Romi?'

'It's still early days,' I say. 'And besides, if anybody's got skinny, it's Nora.'

'It has an impact on your child's brain. The hypothalamus. If you don't eat. I heard them talking about it on the radio the other day. First the kid comes out too small. Cries all the time. Then later it gets fat. Just look at me!' She lifts her T-shirt slightly and points at her stomach.

'That's my mother's doing! Only, she didn't know any better back then.'

'Since when have you had a problem with your weight?' I ask.

'I appreciate every gram of myself,' she says. 'But I haven't always felt like that. Society doesn't like it when women take up space. Or have opinions of their own. And that's putting it mildly. So it was hard-won, all of it.'

She runs her hand over the shiny cloth napkin three times, then carries on. 'What I really want to say is this: it's never too soon to start taking countermeasures against external influence. For most of us, honestly what would be great is if we could influence our genes in the same way as the hypothalamus. Why don't you have some butter with your bread?'

She nudges the little plate towards me.

'Thanks. It's good to eat something,' I say. 'But what you're saying about genes – we give them far too much credit. I mean, you know they can be heavily impacted by our environment and habits, even by our nutrition?'

'Sure,' Szibilla says. 'But your parents affect those things too. Your habits. Your environment.'

'I always thought you had a good relationship with your parents,' I say.

'I did,' Szibilla says. 'But heredity overall is just generally bad! There's no getting round it. Genetics, epigenetics. In the end it all amounts to the same thing. You're still shaped by the history of your parents. Your parents' parents. By the impact they had on this earth. It all gets embedded in your mentality, and you don't even realise. That's why it's important to really think consciously about the world. To really free yourself from those things. And to eat enough. For your baby's sake.'

Szibilla seems larger than before, as though in the time we've been sitting here her body has slowly but surely expanded. I put the rest of the bread into my mouth, chew, swallow. Reach for another slice from the basket.

'Yeah, I feel very similarly about the external influences that shape us,' I say. 'But back to genetics – as I said, you have a lot more control than you think. Which is what you're basically saying yourself.'

'And how about you, Romi?' asks Szibilla.

'How about what?'

'I mean, do you feel like you've ever really confronted the external influences that have shaped you?'

I laugh out loud, but Szibilla's face is serious.

'That's quite some question,' I say. 'As I said, obviously my parents – and everything they did or didn't do – had a more significant impact on me and my life than I'd like. They still do.'

Szibilla shifts in her chair, sitting up straighter. Tilting slightly forward, she asks, 'Your father's affair, for instance, and everything that came with it?'

'Yes, among other things.'

'Correct me if I'm wrong,' Szibilla continues, 'but it wasn't a spontaneous choice on his part, was it, to end the affair?'

I nod. 'After about eighteen months he was pressured into it by my mother. To this day I wonder sometimes what would have happened if she hadn't done that. But why are you so interested, anyway?'

Szibilla reaches for her glass and takes a sip.

'Because I've been asking myself the following,' she says, putting the glass back down in front of her. 'Is it possible that, in a sense, you're in the same position now that your father was then? Only, the external pressure isn't quite as strong yet?'

My mouth is dry from too much bread. The waiter walks past behind Szibilla and I try to flag him down, but he takes no notice of me.

'Is that a yes or a no?' I hear Szibilla ask.

I turn to her again. 'I need water,' I say.

'I'm sure they're bringing it.'

I swallow, but my throat is empty. Try to think of something else, of Robert, my father, of the sight of him alone in a darkened corridor at school, a cloth in his hand. Of the silence that engulfed him, that loneliness.

At that moment my water arrives, along with some cured ham and melon, compliments of the chef. The waiter asks if we're ready for our starters.

Szibilla nods. I hand my plate back and gulp down half the water. Szibilla is stuffing ham into her mouth.

'I really don't think you can draw such simplistic parallels between my dad's affair and my situation today,' I say. 'But yes, of course I'm interested in what was going on in his head at the time, and what effect that choice had on him. I'm also interested in why it always has to be so black and white. Why monogamy at any cost.'

'Firstly: just ask him.' Szibilla says, chewing. 'And secondly: monogamy simply makes sense for most people. It gives a perception of security.'

'A false perception of security, sure,' I say. 'But it's a construct like any other. One that people are constantly trying to rationalise biologically instead of simply acknowledging how restrictive it can be. Instead of opening the whole thing up!'

Szibilla shakes her head almost imperceptibly. 'Either way, you're no less dependent,' she says. 'No matter which way you look at it.'

She cuts the slice of melon in half and puts one half in her mouth. For a few seconds, there we sit, motionless. Szibilla begins to chew. She seems eager, ready to keep drilling down. 'Have you ever considered making yourself more independent? Like Nora?' she continues.

'That sounds a bit cynical,' I say. 'You saw Nora just now!'

Szibilla looks at me as though she's waiting for something. Then she says, 'I told you before, this afternoon. This will pass. It's all part of it.'

I push my empty prosecco glass towards the edge of the table and say, 'And I asked you this afternoon what it is I've failed to notice about Nora over the past couple of months. Maybe you could finally give me an answer?'

Szibilla flicks my glass with her finger: a brief, high, ringing note.

'I did tell you! Nora is in the process of making herself independent. Of Emrik. And not just him,' she goes on. 'And now I'll repeat *my* question: don't you think it would do you good to focus on yourself for a while?'

I can still hear the ringing of the glass. I touch it, but the note lingers, growing louder and more shrill.

I pull myself up and ask, 'Szibilla, what exactly is it you've been wanting to say to me this whole time?'

The waiter is already back at our table, removing Szibilla's empty dish and placing a small salad in front of her.

'Come on, Romi,' she says. 'Don't take this the wrong way. But let's be honest. From what I can see, you like it. Following the norms. Then acting like you're above them. Like you've made some big discovery. And yet you're still in the same old rut!'

'I don't understand what you're talking about.'

'I get the impression that you secretly enjoy it,' Szibilla goes on. 'Being dependent. As a woman. On the perceived security Phil gives you. On Dennis's dick. On Leon's childish affection. But you're such an eloquent speaker that you can frame it differently. You talk about it like you're creating something new. Modern familial relationships? Polyamory? Being dependent on multiple people, that's what I'd call it! Same goes for the money side of things. If it was really important to you to be independent of Phil, you'd be taking a much more pragmatic approach to your career.'

I drink more water. My mouth remains dry.

'Why are you attacking me like this?' I ask.

'You asked me!' Szibilla replies. 'Do you have any painkillers?'

'Painkillers? No.'

'I'm on my last legs here. Back in a second.'

Szibilla gets to her feet and staggers away through the dining room towards the stairs.

I hear the murmuring of people, the jangle of cutlery, the clink of glassware, as if it hadn't all been there already, and I let myself slump down, hands on my belly. I could leave. Out through the sliding door, down the hill to the Rhine. I could jump into the water and swim downstream towards Lake Constance, through the lake, past Basel and onward, north; my father laughs out loud, Robert, he's laughing in my face Stay here, I think, you owe it to Nora, and look, Szibilla's already coming back down. See her powerful legs, her determination, which extends from the pale crown of her head to her black trainers. A waitress overtakes her from behind.

'Right,' Szibilla says when she reaches our table, her voice a little softer now. 'Madame Ibuprofen is back. I'll be feeling better in ten minutes.'

'Are you always this argumentative when you're on your period?' I ask.

'Not argumentative. Direct,' Szibilla says. She sits down and reaches for a slice of bread, the last one in the basket, then launches into her salad, taking big bites. The thought of being served my own food makes my throat constrict.

'Over the past few weeks, I've had a couple of realisations,' Szibilla says. 'I've had this sort of vague feeling for ages, and now I can finally put it into words. I'll give you an example: the women's strike. Nora and you. You come up with slogans. Paint banners. Hand out flyers. Not that I don't see the point, mind you. But the really important stuff goes deeper than that. A lot deeper!'

I get the urge to take out the menu again and study it in detail, purely to avoid being dragged further into this conversation. Instead, I say, 'Are you really this upset that we couldn't go to Berlin? That instead of a relaxing city break you're stuck here with me? Is that the problem?'

I pause, then when Szibilla doesn't reply, I go on: 'Oh, and by the way, Nora is the one who likes to organise stuff, not me.'

'You had a privileged upbringing,' Szibilla says, as though she hasn't heard me. 'Bread and marmalade on the breakfast table every morning so you could go to school on a full stomach. Classrooms where they spoon-fed you everything you needed to learn. You had time to pore over books while your parents earned the money. To make all of this possible for you. And what do you do with this privilege? Instead of using it, instead of pursuing this idea, you make yourself dependent on other people. Just like Nora used to be on that junkie.'

'That's ironic, coming from you, with your posh food and expensive wine, this prosecco.' I point at the bottle. 'How would you live without your mother's inheritance? And the ability to live with your brother?'

Szibilla pauses for a moment. Then, calmly and in a steady voice, she says, 'Those are my little perks. I'd be fine without them.' She clears her throat and continues. 'Unlike you, I'm an active participant in this world.'

'Oh really? In what way?'

'I make an effort to really think about what's going on. To talk to people about it. For instance, why it makes no sense to bring more children onto this planet.'

'And that's your idea of getting involved, is it? A few conversations? And do you harangue Nora with your opinions as well?'

'I've never had to hold back with Nora, actually,' Szibilla says. 'She's been doing the same thing for ages anyway. Overthinking.'

The pressure in my throat is intensifying – it feels as though some frigid object has caught in it.

'Nora's on the right track,' Szibilla continues.

'Slow down,' I say. 'You're making my head swim!'

'Okay, Romi, I'll put it to you another way. You're almost thirty years old. You have a husband. A child. A lover. You're pregnant. You live in a flat Phil inherited. And you're not earning any money of your own. To me that looks like the opposite of liberation.'

A steaming bowl of soup is placed in front of me. A plate before Szibilla. Neither of us touches the food.

'There are so many incredibly important things we could be thinking about,' Szibilla says. 'About the future of this planet! But I guess you don't have time for those questions any more.'

'And how would you know?'

'It doesn't seem like you have the bandwidth for anything except your relationship problems.'

Szibilla reaches for her fork.

'Most relationships aren't much more than an attempt to fill some sort of hole inside you,' she says. 'If one person can't do it, you let another person have a go. But Romi, those holes can never be filled. They're bottomless pits! Don't you want to go one step further than your father did, at the end of his affair? Make a decision before it's too late? Of your own free will?'

'Szibilla, do you even realise how meddlesome you're being right now?'

'Believe me, I only want the best for you,' she says, putting the fork back down, the handle precisely parallel to the napkin. 'Look at it this way. We're here. In this hotel. Together. You can't avoid me. And you certainly can't avoid yourself. This could be an opportunity for you to finally face facts.'

'Sounds like the ex-teacher in you is starting to come out,' I say promptly; Szibilla laughs.

I stare into the soup. It's a yellowish beige, with a blob of fat swimming on the surface. I push the bowl away. I see the steam rise from it, but it's no longer in my nose, and beyond the steam is Szibilla, her pursed lips.

'Is it because you've had bad experiences, is that why you think so negatively?' I ask, persistent.

For a moment Szibilla turns away, as though she's about to get up and leave. Then with a jerk she swivels back in my direction, and her face is as though it has been drawn on thin tissue paper – I've never seen her like that before.

'Don't you think there are any positive examples of relationships?' I ask, a little more calmly.

Now Szibilla is back. She picks up her knife and fork, cuts the cubes of tofu on her plate into halves and says, 'Sure, of course there are. But they're pretty rare.'

She puts the knife back on the table and continues. 'There's something so reactionary about the whole concept of coupledom. Same goes for having children. But children deserve the best. Once they're here.'

'And what's "best" for me, then?' I ask. 'What's "best" for children?'

Szibilla loads a portion of tofu and rice onto her fork and puts it into her mouth. She chews and swallows. Then she says, 'Like I said, you've got to really engage with the problems besetting this world. For yourself, but also as a mother. There are more important things than your relationships!'

'You know something? You remind me of my dad,' I retort. 'You've got the same intransigence, the same pessimism.'

Szibilla raises her eyebrows – she's almost smirking.

'Unlike my father, I'm actually interested in my child,' I say. 'And I hope you're not trying to tell me that meeting Dennis made me less loving towards my son. Do you really think I wanted to move to the village? Do you think I planted strawberries for him because I actually wanted a fucking garden? We live there because Phil's grandmother died and because there are other kids in the building for Leon to play with! And no, I'm obviously not happy about being unemployed with nothing to do but the unpaid job of mothering!'

'See, that's what I mean. Totally dependent,' Szibilla says, continuing to eat unfazed.

'Life is full of compromises and contradictions,' I reply. 'If everybody lived like you, half the human race would have died of loneliness by now.'

Lifting her chin, Szibilla says, 'If everybody lived like me, soon there wouldn't be any people at all. Which would be a good thing.'

'Are you serious?'

'Yes.'

Szibilla takes another forkful of tofu, wipes her mouth with her napkin and continues. 'Aren't you worried that Phil's going to start putting pressure on you soon? Because he's not really okay with this whole situation after all? Because he realises it wasn't a good idea? To share everything. Not just material assets.'

'It's not about that,' I say. 'I was trying to explain how uncomfortable it is living off someone else's money. Regardless of the circumstances.'

'You don't seem to be finding it uncomfortable. If you did, you'd have found a job by now. Even if it wasn't exactly what you wanted, there's always something. But no – your focus is elsewhere. And that's only possible thanks to Phil's salary.'

'It's not that simple,' I say.

'Yes, it is. The principle is extremely simple. Right now, Phil is bringing in the money. You clean. Do the shopping. Grow strawberries. Look after Leon. You're carrying a second child. You could hire someone else to do all that. And you would be paying that person for this work. Currently, Phil is paying you. Indirectly, anyway. That's how your little economic system works. Under the guise of "love". It's a system in which you are dependent on him. And he on you.'

'You do realise there's a bit more to it than that? To women's dependency on men, I mean. Historically speaking.'

'Look, all I can do is repeat myself, Romi. Stop shackling yourself to men. Liberate yourself as much as you possibly can. Not just for yourself, but for your children!'

'What would you know about being a mother anyway?' I say. 'About having a relationship?'

'Well done, Romi. Great way to keep me out of the debate.'

'How are we supposed to have a debate if you keep lumping everything together? Mothers, children, relationships, the whole world. You talk about being free as if you've got it all figured out. But what do you actually mean by that, specifically?'

'I've just explained,' Szibilla says. 'I mean making yourself as independent as possible. From these relationships inherently *based* on dependency.'

'So you think you're freer than me purely because you've chosen to be a lone wolf? That's absurd. And if that's all you've got to say, then I've had enough. And now I'd like to eat my meal!' I say.

'Bon appétit!' Szibilla replies.

I dip my spoon into the soup, which has gone cold by now and tastes of nothing. I swallow and continue spooning. Only once I see the bottom of the bowl do I say, 'It would be nice if you could make at least a rudimentary effort to understand me instead of being so combative all the time.' I put the spoon down on the table. 'And anyway, we're here because of Nora.'

'Nora really needed you these past couple of weeks.'

'Oh, here it comes, the accusation.'

'It's a fact.'

'So why didn't you call me? Text me?'

'Nora didn't want me to.'

'Why not?' I ask.

'I think that would be better coming from her.'

The pressure in my throat is becoming unbearable. 'I can't do this any more,' I say. 'I'm feeling really sick.'

'Let's eat a bit more. Then we'll go back and see Nora. Maybe there's been a new development by now. And you can ask her your question directly.'

'I'd rather leave her be.'

'If you want to leave your comfort zone, sometimes it's going to hurt. You know that.'

'You spend too much time alone, Szibilla.'

'At least it gives me room to breathe,' she says. 'Hang on, I'm just going to grab the pepper mill.'

Szibilla

What a stupid idea. Our idea. All we accomplished by making so much fuss was to flush out Anni. Romi clutching that letter in her hand. We found it outside Nora's bedroom door. The door itself: locked.

Let me be completely clear, Nora had written. *I want to sleep. I didn't ask anybody to come, and I'm not asking anybody to sit by my bedside and hold my hand. I want rest, that's all.*

Romi's horrified face. She stood outside the door, pleading with Nora to open it. To talk to her, just for a minute or two! I left her to it. Romi turned to me. Said, 'And you're just going to stand there, are you?'

Yes. I respected Nora's wishes. What was the point of making such a hullabaloo? She'd only clam up even tighter.

Anni was at the bottom of the stairs in seconds. Snapping at us. What did we think we were doing, making all that noise? Were we trying to wake Meret? Romi did her best to placate her, asking if she'd read the note. Had there been any other changes? Anni read Nora's scribble. Again and again, she shook her head. 'There it is in black and white,' she said. Nora needed her rest – and so did Anni. Then she hustled us out.

On our walk back to the hotel, Romi didn't say a word. Not until we went our separate ways. She needed some time alone. All of the next day, she said, unless Nora called. Was I staying too? Or would I leave? Of course I'd stay, I assured her.

Romi went up to her room. I stayed out another hour or so to take a walk. The valley seemed more tranquil than it had by day, despite the inconstant light of the street lamps. Beyond the lamps, the mountains. And above those, the milky sky. Darkening, slowly.

Whatever it is that's troubling Nora, it must be more deep-seated than I thought. Tomorrow we shall see. See if anything changes. If she decides to emerge from her shell. To speak, frankly. That's what Nora's like – it's what our friendship is like. With Nora I have never had to hide. Nor she from me.

Upstairs, I lie down. One final pill. A mouthful of water. Sleep will come.

DAY TWO

9 June

Romi

I can see black rectangles, dots, circles; between them, an order-bringing white. I'm lying on the floor, the green carpet. I've been dreaming. I raise my head, drool trailing from my lips to the inscription in my notebook: *Berlin. The Capital*. Beside it is the lead pencil, its tip pointing to the printed map, to what symbolises streets and squares. Where is all this going to lead? I was outside, in a field, striking the earth again and again, enraged because I didn't have the strength to flatten the ground. Eventually I let myself fall forward, into a hollow that appeared suddenly – upper body first, then legs. The hollow filled with water, and I realised someone else was there, although I couldn't make out who. A tremor; I surfaced. The notebook in front of me, a gift from Dennis. I had found it the day before yesterday, early in the morning, lying on my clothes. *Berlin. The Capital.* And now I'm in the Rhine Valley. How did I get to this place, this floor, this grimy carpet, alone? What drove Nora here, what's happening with her? It can't be all that early, seven o'clock or a few minutes after that; I pick myself up, heavy-boned, and lie down in the bed. In the notebook, still here, between its leaves: Nora's letter.

I write. The last page of the book, the very last blank page.

NOTE

Number of words in Nora's letter: twenty-eight.

The piece of paper in my hand yesterday, and the hand shaking, and Szibilla
so calm-seeming, as though she knew already what was coming. The look fixed
on me: full of disdain.

As if I was to blame, but to blame for what? To blame for Nora lying there,
for the fact that she's hit rock bottom?

Number of meetings with Szibilla in the last 103 days: two.

Of those, the number without Nora: one. Fourteen days ago.

She rushed past us in the supermarket – she's here, in town? –
then spun round abruptly, looking first at Leon, then at Dennis,
then at me. A cursory hello, then she had to be on her way, off
to the DIY and Garden department to pick up some paint. They
were decorating Nora's new flat. She'd come in specially. She was
swinging her shopping basket back and forth as an apple rolled
from one side to the other, rustling the paper bag that wrapped
the bread.

'What flat?' I asked.

'Didn't she tell you?' Szibilla asked in reply.

'What?'

'Nora's moved out.'

'Of Emrik's place?'

'Where else?'

'I had no idea!'

'She's got her own flat again. Same place she lived before,
above the swimming pool.'

'She's back on Badstraße? In her old studio?'

'Better. This one's got a separate bedroom. She's done it,
finally,' Szibilla said, before adding that she had to be off. They
wanted to make the most of the time. Meret was with her dad.
With Emrik.

And when Szibilla repeated the name, as if I was ignorant not just of the move but also of the fact that 'Emrik' and 'Meret's dad' were one and the same person, she stopped the movement of her arm. The apple came to a halt in the middle of the basket. Then she swept away, her backside bobbing up and down in the black jogging bottoms she always likes to wear.

'That was Szibilla?' Dennis asked, when she was out of sight behind the shelves.

'That was Szibilla,' I replied, then I fell quiet. We paid for our shopping, for the punnet of organic strawberries that Dennis was buying for Leon. So Nora had done it, then, whatever that meant.

Outside, at the bus stop, Dennis asked me what was wrong, cupping my head in both hands, kissing me. I pulled away. Too soon to display ourselves like this, in public. He took a step back and leant against the side of the bus shelter, hands in his jacket pockets, dark hair shiny as brilliantine. Half a metre too much between him and me. Leon, sitting on the bench in the shelter, stuffed one strawberry after another into his mouth as he watched the traffic go by.

'I don't understand why Nora didn't tell me,' I said to Dennis.

'Give her a call,' he said, as a worried crease appeared between his brows.

I shook my head. 'Tomorrow. She'll be busy today,' I said, and put out my arm to touch Dennis's forehead. Our bus drew up. I took Leon's hand. 'I'm sorry to disappoint you. That I don't have the courage to be seen with you in public yet,' I added to Dennis as I got on.

'It's okay,' he said behind me. 'I told you – I'm following you into the labyrinth.'

Turning to him, I saw on his lips an astonishingly shy smile, and then I kissed him after all, once, on the lips, forgetting for a moment the people around us, forgetting Szibilla and what she had told me about Nora.

The green of the carpet in this room is the same as yesterday, but I'm only noticing today that the colour isn't even: it's more intense at the edges and scuffed towards the middle of the room, by the bed. There's my bag. I dig out my phone and open the chat with Nora. I texted her on 26 May, morning, one day after bumping into Szibilla. *Everything okay? Do you want to chat on the phone? I heard you're making big changes! Excited to hear all the details!* :-*

Her response arrived the same day, but not until evening: *Hey! Yep! I'm back on Badstraße, hopefully getting some freedom back as well. I'll be in touch. Got a few things to work through (alone). Big hugs.*

I answered fifteen minutes later: *Okay, well call me as soon as you have time and space and fancy a housewarming drink. Would be lovely. Je t'aime!*

And then nothing else, which wasn't unusual for Nora, and I didn't push.

There was something I didn't see for what it was, something I missed. I was sulking, absorbed, so far away from Nora. I can see her now before me, at Buena Onda in mid-April. Her hair glowed as though charged with red light, her voice rose above everything else, cracking as she talked about the trip to Berlin, about the long weekend. 'I'll get the train tickets,' she announced, then surveyed my still-flat stomach and said, 'A change of air for a day or two. That's what we need.'

'You know what I need?' I asked, giving her a look of mock defiance.

'Yes. You need to mix things up a bit,' Nora answered, sounding unusually matter-of-fact. 'And you need a crop top for the summer, let the little one get a bit of sun.'

'If that's all,' I say, 'then fine.'

Nora fidgeted, as though trying to shake something off, then sat up straighter. The summer collection had arrived at Boutique Chic a few days ago, she said, and the trending colour this season was Living Coral. Apparently, this was a political statement. Every year, an American institute selected its Color of the Year, and this year's choice was supposed to draw attention to global warming, to the dying coral reefs and the environmental protection they so desperately needed. 'Load of absolute bullshit,' she said.

Immediately Szibilla jumped on the idea, saying this was just an example of a common problem, more meaningless virtue-signalling. 'It's the same with feminism, isn't it?'

'Yeah, totally!' said Nora, strangely eager. 'Did I tell you they're printing "Our Minds, Our Bodies, Our Power" onto these shitty coral T-shirts? They'll be available at the bigger shops next week. We won't be stocking them at Boutique Chic, of course, out of consideration for the over-sixties, because for them that's a bridge too far. They prefer something simple, they don't want that stuff shoved in their faces!'

Nora rolled her eyes, and I was tempted to ask why she was still working at the boutique, why she hadn't quit that job long ago and resumed her studies. Meret was getting too old to be a good excuse for why she hadn't finished. But I missed my chance, because Szibilla was already asking whether Nora was trying to say that women over sixty weren't welcome at her Women's Strike.

'*My* Women's Strike?' Nora asked. She paused, then went on: 'Of course they are! I'm just talking about the Boutique Chic ladies. Let's say 93 per cent of the women who come through our doors, at a rough estimate.'

Then she promptly returned to the trending colour of the season. She said that the very same day she had put everything but this Living Whatever colour into the window display, and had immediately been hauled over the coals by her boss. Still, the colour itself wasn't bad, she added. In fact, it would suit me. There was a top in the boutique that she was thinking of giving me for my birthday – but then again, I didn't want to celebrate that.

'Why not, though? Why haven't we learned to celebrate things *nicely*?' she asked, emphasis on the *nicely*. Looking first at Szibilla then at me, she went on, switching abruptly to the topic of her own birthday, her twenty-eighth. She never wanted to celebrate like that again, she said, with Emrik's group of friends, never again, spending the whole night in that crazy boozy soup. Next time she wanted it to be *nice*.

'What do you mean by "nice"?' Szibilla asked. 'Raising a glass with Empress Sissi at Trauttmansdorff Castle?'

'Haha.' Nora's voice was dark and far from cheerful. She said, 'Anything is better than puking my guts out with Emrik and his bunch of idiots.'

Then she changed the subject again, returning to her job and the generally lousy pay in the fashion industry, how at twenty-eight you're already ancient as a model – but who'd be a model in this world anyway? Recently she'd been scrolling through a series of photos online entitled: Celeb Mums Show Off Their Pretty Daughters; or, Nora's subtitle: The Apple Doesn't Fall Far from the Tree – Unfortunately for the Apple.

Nora tapped away on her phone then held out the screen to us. On it was a photograph of a girl clutching an umbrella with both hands and peering through thick glasses with a faint squint. The caption: 'It's hard to believe this young lady is just seven years old.' Then a second photo, the same child in her mother's arms, both wearing French braids. The woman was blowing an air kiss at the camera, and underneath the picture it said: 'Kim Kardashian's eldest daughter already knows how to pose for the camera.'

'That kind of cynicism makes me sick,' said Nora, putting her phone back into her bag and murmuring, 'Hopefully Meret can put as much distance between me and her as possible. In every possible way.'

'What do you mean?' I asked, but Nora was already talking again, now addressing me. She didn't understand my problem with turning thirty – it was such a beautiful number, she told me, I of all people should appreciate that. Three, zero, elegant.

'Anyway,' she said, 'with every year that goes by, you become more independent of the places you come from. More independent of the people you grew up with.'

For a moment she was still, almost as though frozen. Film over, curtain down. Then life slowly flickered back and Nora said, softly now, 'Every now and then I dream about the Rhine. Load of bullshit really. Why the Rhine? Anyway. Now I have to pee.'

I went with her to the toilet. As we stood at the basin, Nora's hands under the tap, I asked her at long last what was going on. Had something happened – was there something on her mind? Nora drew her hands back; the water stopped. There was a shift in the angle of the light across her face as she leant towards me, her hair an ecstatic plane of red, a landscape all its own. Instead of answering me, she said, 'I envy you, you know that?'

I hugged her clumsily, as if I hadn't done it a thousand times before, and with my lips very close to her ear I asked her what she meant. Nora pulled back. Our faces were now only a few centimetres apart; I could smell the coffee on her breath and the mingled acrid scent of hair dye. Her skin seemed paler than before, her contours vague, as though she was vanishing and occupying space at the same time. She was the seventeen-year-old I had known long ago, walking into the classroom, sitting down in Vural's seat and throwing the whole system into disarray.

'I wish I could do what you do,' she said. 'Just go ahead and prioritise my needs. Liberate myself. But I've lost the knack.'

The toilet door opened and somebody shuffled into the tiny space. Nora disentangled herself and went back up the stairs to where Szibilla sat. When I got back, Nora was already on her way out, and we haven't said a word about it since. I've felt as though she's been avoiding me, and my own days have been dictated by nausea and children and talking, talking, talking. At first I kept trying to get hold of her, then less and less, and after 26 May I gave up, pinning my hopes on Berlin, on the days we would spend together there, a point of convergence.

I run my hand over the notebook. *Berlin. The Capital.* As though the city has shrunk to fit this section of map – while my own inner map has shrunk as well. There aren't many places, many streets where I spend time these days. The places where I sit or lie, where I can rest, are heavily circled: Dennis's bed, my reading chair, my seat on the train. The paths between them are dashed lines, thin: from the village train station up the hill by bike, back down again with Leon, to the nursery, the village shop, and then back up again to snatch an hour or two at my desk; I go around the flat with my cleaning supplies, stove on, stove off; I head out into the garden with my hoe and then I'm back off to the station, boarding a train into town for a supermarket shop, for an appointment at the gynaecologist, for a date with Dennis. Seven o'clock, nine o'clock, twelve o'clock, five o'clock, ten o'clock. My guilt has disgorged itself into street corners and into the nooks and crannies of the lanes, a viscous ink, greasy and tenacious, and shame has rounded the corners of my inner map just as it has rounded my back. Traces of ink in my and Phil's bed, on the sofa, at the dining table. Yet not a single word of reproof from him.

And nothing from Nora.

Still nothing. I put my phone on the carpet, as far away as possible, and stay lying in bed like a foetus, like the foetus in my belly, like Nora yesterday, silent on her ninety-centimetre mattress. I knew nobody better than Nora. And she no one better than me. There was no one I wanted to be more than her. At first, when I was eighteen. Later I was just happy to be spending time with her. At nineteen. And twenty. While she was twirling across the dance floor and I was in her wake, both with vodka Red Bull in our hands and in our blood; while after hours of dancing and talking and bellowing one of us suggested going back to Nora's, to her studio flat, and the two of us – or sometimes three or four of us – would end up on her bed, passing a joint from hand to hand; from female hand to female hand. *Just Between Us*, Nora used to call these get-togethers, after the old German soap, which we had long since stopped watching and which depicted the opposite of the world she wanted to live in. I loved those hours in her flat, the view from her bed onto the balcony, where there was always a bin bag, always full to bursting, and next to it, on the step, an ashtray made of reddish glass.

One notebook is full. The second is heavier. I open it. The pages are smoother than in the other, and the pencil glides more easily.

NOTE

Number of cigarettes we smoked during our first breaktime together behind the hazel bush, Nora and I: two each.
Number of hours we had known each other by then: two and a half.
Her first day at our school, my third year.

She exuded something utterly unlike what I was used to. She was so completely of the world yet so outside it: a cosmos of her own, an island. The moment I first saw her, with her black-dyed pixie cut and heavy fringe, the denim bag over her shoulder and the defiant, animated face, I dropped anchor. She saved me.

She was the first person I told, quite openly, without feeling ashamed of it – it was one of the first things I said to her, in fact – 'I live in the school building.'

She replied, 'And I live in the Rhine Valley. Pretty much the same thing.'

I asked her what she meant.

She bored a hole in a hazel leaf with her lit cigarette and said, 'They're both too fucking small.'

I told her I'd grown up under our schoolhouse roof, smelling the mop water and the polish on my father's clothes, the chalk and watercolours on my mother's hands, and that as soon as I left the family home and entered the school corridors, I could smell the cold concrete, the children's slippers, and I went to the library as often as I could. I would wander among the bookshelves, early mornings mostly, when the school was still quiet, and I'd take out a book here and there, read a few lines, arrange them into new and loose conjunctions, and something in me could breathe again. That silence was bearable, beautiful even. I could nestle into it, because it stood up to the weight – unlike the silence in our flat, which clung to the walls like cigarette smoke, a silence that had begun to wedge itself between my parents when I was eleven.

Nora was the first person I told: my father was six foot three and a school caretaker; my mother was five foot one and started teaching primary school when I hit puberty. Both had once been into yoga, secretly, because in those days it did not belong at school, not even a school in a city, and both had promised each other lifelong fidelity. A promise my father couldn't keep.

'He was faithful to me until he couldn't manage it. And he couldn't manage it for about a year and a half,' my mother sometimes said to people afterwards, friends, relatives, and whenever she said it my palms would begin to sweat. She sounded so casual, like she was chatting about her last shopping trip or some exam, but I could tell how hurt she was. It was present in everything my mother did.

Nora didn't probe that first day, and I told her I was an in-be-tweener. Not bad at sports and not bad at sitting still; not too loud and not too quiet; rarely too early and never too late; not too noisy and not too silent. An only child. Close neither to my mother nor to my father. A teacher's kid. An average kid. I was five foot eight, I said, and likely to stay that way.

'You don't get to decide when it comes to that shit,' Nora said, and I leant against her, feeling her bare stomach through my shirt and putting my finger on her belly-button piercing as though it were mine.

'It's new,' Nora said, she'd had it done recently, on the day she'd moved out of her mother's house – or rather, had been moved out of it.

I asked what that meant. Nora only said, 'That's just the way it is, parents are stingy. Yours. Mine *definitely*. And I'm not talking about money.'

She told me that her mother was paying for a studio flat in the city for her, almost four hundred francs a month, and that she was able to eat thanks to regular signs of life from her father, which had been arriving exclusively via bank transfer for the last three years.

At that moment the school bell rang, but we stayed sitting there, Nora and I, for another half an hour, as though we took it for granted we would draw out breaktime as long as we liked, as though nothing else concerned us any more. Nora said the house she grew up in was a perpetual building site, at least one of the rooms always under construction. There were draughts here and draughts there as windows were replaced, floors laid, roofs insulated, walls torn down, carpets switched for laminate. Only her room had remained untouched. It was the only room in the house that had stayed virtually unchanged since her parents moved in seventeen years earlier, shortly before Nora was born.

In the old days she had thought her father left her room alone because he wanted to give her some peace and quiet, Nora said. Or because every time he got around to it, he was distracted by some other room that needed renovating, one where the call was more pressing. He had rarely lingered long in her room at all. It was her mother who shook her awake in the morning and chivvied her to bed at night.

'My dad was a corner-seat friend, a balcony friend,' said Nora. 'He smoked and talked pretty much non-stop. I loved hanging out with him. But then he left, quite suddenly.'

And when he walked out, Nora realised something: she had been fooled. The reason why, in all those years, he had touched nothing in her room was because he knew that the holes he would ultimately leave in her life could never be spackled over.

Nora paused, then said, out of the blue, 'I like the way you make the smoke ripple.'

Did her dad leave for another woman, I wanted to know? By then I was wishing mine had done the same, instead of leaving the job half finished.

'I don't know anything about that,' Nora said, and asked in what way I thought things might improve without my dad.

I said it would have cleared things up, at least. That my parents and I had stuck together after the end of his affair yet had little to do with each other as a family, really, for three whole years – years in which both parents kept themselves as busy as possible.

My mother was still doing her course and my father would sit and meditate all evening long for months, a Celtic Tree Calendar pinned to the wall in front of him. Meanwhile I had tried to hold the threads together, to unknot them, but the next day I would pick them up and entwine my parents yet again, draw them into conversation: about school, my friends, the guinea pig. What mattered was to talk.

'When did they split up?' asked Nora, and I said, 'That's just it. They didn't.'

She nodded and said it sounded awful, although personally she'd had a worse time when it was just her and her mum. After her dad left, her mum only had Nora, apart from her office job, and instead of living her own life she had kept a close watch on everything her daughter did, nagging endlessly. 'A pigsty', she used to call Nora's room.

Nora laughed, and this laugh, a little too grating, too long, clasped itself against the harshness of the word 'pigsty'. I heard the laugh again that same day, after school, when we entered Nora's brand-new studio flat and I gestured in astonishment at the shiny black lettering above her bed. *Pigsty*, it read.

NOTE

Number of years our friendship has lasted: twelve.
Number of people who have been as close to me as Nora: two.
Number of flats Nora has occupied since moving out of her mum's: a dozen. But only two of them for more than six months.
1) *The room on Badstraße, upstairs from the public baths where she did her lengths every day, up and down the pool.*
2) *Later on, the hole where Emrik lived, before the recent move back to Badstraße.*

'The good into the pot, the bad into the crop,' Nora said before the meal she gave me on our first night in the pigsty, serving it as ceremoniously as if it were a formal dinner: bread and cheese on a gilt-edged plate from a junk shop. She lit another cigarette and opened a beer.

'Do you like fairy tales?' I asked.

'Do you like beer?' was her reply.

I nodded. She opened another bottle for me. Her mum had read her fairy tales occasionally, she said, but they were far from her best memories. She had no idea why the line about the pot and the crop had just materialised in her head.

Then, unexpectedly, she said, 'The train journey from here to my mum's is forty-five minutes. I'm glad of every metre between us. How can you bear to still live with your parents, Romina?'

I took an embarrassed sip of my lukewarm beer and said I usually did my own thing, and my parents left me in peace. Horseshit, Nora replied. They were bound to be watching everything, and I just hadn't got wise to it.

Then she went on, in a serious tone of voice, 'I *never* want kids. It's so gross the way they slobber and shit themselves and they're always needing something. The way they stare at you and purr like cats, like they're always expecting something. From Mum, from Dad, from the world. And they get it, too, because despite it all, people still think they're cute. Then they get older and step on their parents' toes and their parents step on theirs. Honestly, I really have no idea why people do it to themselves. I made up my mind ages ago. I want freedom.'

And after a moment's pause she added, 'A life that's all my own.'

Then she popped a tiny piece of cheese into her mouth and asked, 'Do you mind if I call you Romi?'

NOTE

Coming – going. Staying – leaving. Being free – being unfree. A decision for – a decision against. 'A life that's all my own', as if there were any such thing.
Number of seconds it takes for a decision already taken to filter into the conscious mind: seven.
Number of seconds it takes before that decision is followed by an action: one.
- *Go up to Nora, ask her for a cigarette, become Romi.*
- *Meet Phil at a school reunion after a long time has passed, talk to him the whole night, four years later have a kid with him. Be a mother.*
- *Get into a conversation in a café, say 'yes' that same night, lie in bed with Dennis, room 217.*

Susan Sontag said: 'Most everything I do seems to have as much to do with intuition as with reason. It isn't that love presupposes comprehension, but to love somebody is to be involved in all kinds of thoughts and judgments. That's what it is – there's an intellectual structure of physical desire, of lust.

Sigmund Freud said that in small matters you should trust the mind, and in the large ones, the gut.

Nine-oh-one. I can smell my own sour perspiration. Pulling my shirt off over my head, I wash my armpits in the bathroom basin, avoiding the mirror. I dig a fresh top out of my rucksack. Still nothing from Nora. I wish I could go back, be out there on the dance floor with her, dance away all the shittiness in our lives, as Nora used to say, her voice darkened by the cigarettes. When did nights like that become less frequent?

I want to see Nora, I want to lie down next to her and ask her, does she? Does she regret anything about Meret's birth or her decisions in general? I want to ask if that's what's tormenting her so badly now. If this decision to opt out is her finally beginning to assert her own needs again – only, too late.

I want to. I want to. To ask myself if I'm actually liberating myself, like Nora said, or the opposite, like Szibilla thinks. Asserting my needs, but at what cost? Phil in front of me when I told him about Dennis and me, the way a mix of pain, astonishment and dullness spread across his face, a mix that came to settle over the relationship as a whole, over the family, like a scab over a wound.

'But think about how badly your dad's affair hurt you,' was one of the first things Phil said.

And I didn't have an answer for him. I held his gaze until I couldn't any more and covered my face with my hands. I said, 'I'm sorry!'

'For who?'

'For you. For Leon. For us,' I said. 'What do you want from me right now?'

'Nothing,' Phil said. 'Do what you think is right.'

My tears had begun to flow, I couldn't help it, and I said, 'My feelings for you are as strong as ever!'

Phil stood up and said he couldn't do this right now, he had to be alone for a while.

NOTE

How did Robert feel about it, at the time?
He never said he regretted choosing us, even if he hadn't chosen freely, even if Mum had badgered him into it.
He never said he was happy about it either.

Number of words he ever expended on all this: zero.
Number of times I asked him about it directly: one.
I know nothing about my father's decisions, and little enough about him, really.
Nothing about his deepest wishes. Nothing about his regrets.
A silence has descended upon him. This silence even extends to me.

And Nora's silence?

Nine thirteen, battery at 51 per cent. A vacuum cleaner switches on in the corridor; the display goes black again. I feel like calling Nora to ask if she's thinking about Meret, at all, about how her daughter's doing. The vacuum switches off, and I hear voices, two women exchanging a few words. A door is opened.

No, I should talk to Robert. I should get his perspective. Whether he was trying to spare me something – me, his child – by setting aside his own needs. Whether his needs were of a different nature than had occurred to me all these years, what it meant for him, to free himself.

My stomach rumbles dully. I put my hand on my belly: it is sunken underneath the ribs, empty. I move my hand further down, until I reach the small, compact ball above my pubic bone: the place it's growing, the baby.

Szibilla

'There's nothing better than biting into a lemon before breakfast. Rouses the spirit!'

Malita turns to me. The citrus oil is already out. From her I would take anything, including chewed gum. She opens the bin with her foot. Tosses the gum inside. Washes her hands. 'Where I grew up, there were lemon trees every which way you looked.'

'Spain?'

She makes a motion of the head that I can't interpret. Then points towards the table, which is covered with a cloth. I lie down. The disposable knickers are cutting in between my labia. 'Vulval lips,' Nora would correct me. I shuffle forwards, squashing my face into the hole. Malita dispenses the oil. She starts with my upper back. Palms squelching. She asks, 'Is that good?'

I answer, 'I don't know why I'm here either.'

She pauses briefly, asks, 'Too much pressure?'

'In this country, I mean.'

Her hands glide upwards, to the left and right of my spine.

'You could try the Botanical Gardens,' she says. 'Pep up your day, give yourself some time to de-stress. You said it yourself, yesterday: "Too much work, too many loads of laundry." Right?'

Mucus has dislodged. I swallow it.

'I'm going away in the autumn. Quite a long trip, with a friend. She's having a tough time at the moment too.'

'To the south?' Malita asks.

'Probably.'

She adds more oil. Nora might like my plan. It would do her good. Her and me. Like the old days. Liguria. 'I grew up in the Algarve, actually, for a few years when I was little,' she says. 'Portugal.'

Her hands are making small movements. Gentle. Yet with a pleasant pressure.

'Do you like your job?' I ask.

Her hands are now cupping my skull. As if from far away I hear her say, 'Words you can use to disguise yourself, but the body doesn't work that way. This is a mercilessly honest business.'

My head is growing warm. Again those tiny, pulsing movements.

'It's the same with my job,' I say. 'An honest business. And soon there won't be so much stress on my back. The retirement home is being renovated, including the laundry. So no more bending down.'

Malita is working on my upper vertebrae. As though testing something.

'You must really be fond of the old people to be doing the washing for them,' she says. Is that irony in her voice? I find myself liking her more and more.

'It's straightforward enough work,' I reply. 'Purely functional. And that's the beauty of it. Like with you, right?'

'I don't think of you as a dirty towel!' Malita says.

She laughs. Shrilly, almost. Genuine amusement.

'But in principle this is a straightforward service too,' I say. 'Very different from, say, a job in politics.'

'A straightforward service? Now you underestimate me. What I do is very similar to psychological counselling, only its effect is more immediate – and more hidden.'

'And what does that look like?'

She mulls this over. Still massaging. Then she says, 'Take Donald Trump as an example. He's about to impose punitive tariffs on Mexico because the border wall isn't working out the way he'd hoped. If I had Trump on my table right now, I'd end up with cramp in my fingers afterwards and he'd be covered in bruises, because the by-products of what he's done, the dross, would be buried so deep in his fascia that it would take an incredible amount of strength to reach it.'

Her hands are between my shoulder blades. She's pressing down with all her weight. Squeezing all the air out of me.

'But I do reach it, the dross. People's stupidities, that's another way of putting it, but I don't mean that in a nasty way, because getting to their stupidities also means getting to their pain. And when that happens, it's magic!' She pronounces the word with a long, strident *ah*. Pauses. Then: 'If I got my hands on Trump I'd knead out all the crackpot ideas along with the dross. He'd be a different person once he stood back up. If he still could. Get up, I mean.'

Malita draws back her hands. My lungs refill with air.

'Then he could shove his wall up his arse,' I say.

'He'd pull it down with his own two hands, at least the parts that are already up, and he'd be weeping while he did it, because he'd feel so stupid.'

'And what do you have in mind for me?' I ask.

'Don't worry, stupidity isn't your problem. Only pain. And I can take care of that. There it is,' she says, tapping a finger between my shoulder blades, 'and there. Deep down.' Her hands glide down to one of my lower vertebrae.

'Period pain,' I say. 'I always get that.'

'I thought so.'

'I'd like to have the whole lot out, really. All the female giblets. Then I'd slap them down on the front step of some IVF clinic.'

Malita laughs again. Like I was joking. Then she carries on with her massage. My lower back. A wider surface now. More tender.

'Are you serious?' she asks at last.

I try to nod. My head is firmly anchored in the headrest. Malita clicks her tongue.

'Oh, but there are other methods! You're lucky you found me. I'll sort out your pain. But cautiously, okay? We're already working on it. Or are you telling me you don't feel better than yesterday?'

'A bit.'

'You'll see. It just takes time. And now I want you to relax. No talking and no thinking for an hour,' she says. She finds particular areas of my sides to work on, as if she were reaching directly into me. It's a nice idea, kneading out the toxins. It does at least mellow my line of thought. It's not so bad, this torpor in my head.

Romi

The dining room is full again. It smells of breakfast: filter coffee, fresh bread, fried bacon. My stomach turns. I take a bread roll and make my way back down the corridor: a simple labyrinth.

In my room the notebook is where I left it, on the floor beside the bed. As though waiting for something, for me to find words, to sort and order them. For me to get to the bottom of things. Nora in my mind's eye again, so lifeless on her mattress. How many seconds passed between her decision to submerge herself, to break away, and the action that followed? Was it intuitive or calculated, weighed-up — like Robert's had been, maybe?

I pick up the notebook and lie down in bed. The pencil is somewhere underneath the rumpled bedclothes.

NOTE

Reasons I'm aware of why it felt so obvious to say yes to Dennis 103 days ago, in room 217: ...
Number of minutes I spent considering whether to say yes or no: two or three.
Number of minutes I spent waiting for Dennis: fifteen.
Number of minutes that passed between his arrival and the moment he was next to me in bed: half.
Number of hours that passed before the decision reached my conscious mind, until I felt guilt, and shame: four.
Options I'd had, my range of decisions:
— Say no, i.e. send Dennis away
— Just talk to him, leave it at that
— Not rush into anything

– *Run away with Dennis, walk out of my old life into a new one*
– …

I get under the duvet. Much too hot. I take the cover off it and simply pull the fabric over me like a second skin.

Robert in his garden chair, March sun on his face, eyes squinting, when he said those few words: 'You don't see happiness when it's right in front of your face.'

He moved and bumped against the table, slopping foam over the rim of his open beer can, although it didn't seem to bother him. He crossed his arms over his gut, which had grown round since they moved to the suburbs. It rose and fell steadily, unfaltering.

'Whose happiness are you talking about?' I blurted. '*Yours*, maybe? The happiness of being indecisive?'

'We can't talk to each other like that,' Robert said, eyes now fixed straight ahead, as though scanning his distant vegetable patch for weeds in need of pulling.

'We've barely talked for ages anyway!' I said, jumping to my feet. The chair fell with a clatter to the ground behind me. I went off home before my mother was even back from work, leaving Robert to sit in his idyllic garden, with his contented belly.

NOTE

Number of times I have seen Robert in the last 103 days: one.
Number of years since I stopped calling him 'Dad': twelve.
Number of years since my parents moved out of the flat at school: five.
Number of years they've been acting like a happy couple again: nearly fifteen.
Number of moments I've believed them: zero.
Number of hobbies they share today: three. Qi gong, cycling, gardening.

I take a bite of bread roll. Salt on my tongue, saliva pooling. A wave of nausea. I take another bite. Then I feel better. I should call Leon, see what he got up to with Phil's parents this morning, whether they went to the playground or back to see the llamas. His voice, close. But how do I know he's not doing exactly what I used to do myself: fill silence with babble, because I – his mother – am as unreachable as my parents were to me? How do I know that Leon won't eventually try to clutch the threads together as convulsively as I did? Will there be a day when he finds it as impossible to speak to me as I do to my own parents? Will he, too, think only that I made the wrong decision, that I wasn't there for him enough, and will he see in me a woman who forced herself into a corset she had labelled 'happiness'?

I picture Nora and myself, a photograph shortly after we met, taken in the pigsty with a self-timer: our heads are visible in the bottom left-hand corner against the white plaster wall, our faces turned towards each other. We are grinning. Nora seems to be in motion, a lock of hair on the verge of falling forward. It is written in our faces: nothing is impossible, yet.

I recognise that look from Robert: a different picture. He is sitting on the bathroom floor in his underwear and vest, a bottle of baby oil beside him on the beige tiles. I am lying on his outstretched legs, my baby's body glistening. His large hands are resting on my tummy as he looks into the camera, roguish, eager. Nothing is impossible, yet. He could study philosophy or biology. He could emigrate to England or New Zealand. In that picture he must be about the same age I am now, and those plans have long since flown the coop, have diminished and divided.

I take out my phone. The dark screen reflects my face: I look dishevelled, my fringe messy, my lips a line, the corners of my mouth downturned; so, I am that sort of woman. I let my head fall back, listening to a car pass by outside, a whoosh that intensifies then fades; then comes another one. I sit up, switch on my phone. 10.24 a.m. I dial Robert's number, press the phone to my ear. It rings three times before he picks up, and I hear his dull, quick 'Yes?'

'It's me, Romi,' I say. My heart is pounding, almost leaping out of my chest.

'Romina. It's you.'

His voice sounds hoarse, as if he hasn't spoken yet today.

'Has something happened?' he asks. 'How's Leon?'

'Good, I think. He's at home.'

'You're not with him?'

'No,' I say. 'I'm away.'

I hesitate. I can hear the silence between us: the silence that makes me very small. I put my hand on my chest. Better now.

'Are you still there?' I ask. Robert clears his throat. That's all. And suddenly I break it, the silence, I simply start to talk, about the Beech Hotel, about my room and how I'm looking at a view over a farm, how I've been wondering since yesterday what smells so rank, but that it should be obvious, really: it's a pigsty. Now it clicks. I laugh, mostly out of astonishment with myself because it took me this long to realise, and Robert asks, 'What is it?'

'I'm starting to understand things, bit by bit,' I say, regaining my composure, 'but it's still pretty foggy here.'

He coughs again, then says something about the Rhine Valley, about a museum on the Austrian side that explains the history of the Rhine. Have I been there yet? And I say, 'Actually, I wanted to ask why you stayed. Back then, I mean.'

'Stayed?'

'Yeah. I'm talking about the decision you made about the affair. Or whatever you call it. With Tana. Or was her name Dana? Diana?'

Silence on the other end of the line.

'Did you do it for me?'

'Yes, of course,' Robert answers promptly. 'And for your mother. She couldn't live like that. It was long overdue.'

'So it was a kind of sacrifice you made for us?'

He seems to consider this. 'No. It was just the best thing for all concerned.'

I wait.

'It wasn't the best thing for me,' I say. 'For me it was very painful, the three years when you and Mum barely said a word to each other. Then suddenly everything just gets forgotten. You still didn't seem happy to me, you know, even though you were pretending.'

He says nothing, and I ask, 'Would you have split up with Tana if Mum hadn't pressured you into it?'

I can hear Robert breathing heavily. 'Leaving you and your mum was never an option. Anything outside of that was something else. It had nothing to do with your mum. For me.'

'But what was it you were trying to find in Tana?' I ask.

'Let's drop it, okay. It was decades ago! You should be thinking of your own family instead of dwelling on ancient history.'

I swallow. Then I say, 'I'd like to tell you about a memory, okay?'

I take his silence as a yes.

'Do you remember when we went on holiday to the farm?' I begin. 'I would have been about eleven. On the farm there was this pony we wanted to ride. It kept bucking, and it wouldn't take a single step no matter how hard I tried to get it moving. You held a bag of stale bread in front of its nose, then you put it in the basket of your bike and rode away, and the pony galloped after you. I nearly fell out of the saddle, but after the initial shock it was wonderful. You on the bike in front of me. You turned your head and grinned at me.'

Robert says nothing.

'And then all at once you were so silent. It was like something in you had switched off,' I went on.

'You young people don't know what you want,' he says, impatient now. 'That's the problem with your generation. You spend far too much time thinking about things instead of really getting to grips with your lives.'

'Is it really so wrong to question things?'

'You kids don't want to grow up.'

'What do you mean?'

'In the old days you could still rely on things.'

I get to my feet. Gaze out through the window at the farm. 'I'm just trying to understand,' I say.

Again I hear his heavy breath, then he says, 'I think it's a shame you can't just be happy that we repaired our relationship. Your mother and I.'

I turn away from the window and look into the darkness of the room, squint, and spot the notebook on the bed, partially underneath the bedding, and I say, 'I'm sorry. I asked the questions the wrong way. I'd better hang up.'

He is quiet. Then Robert asks, 'Shall I give your love to Mum?'

'Yeah.'

I get into bed and let my phone fall to the floor. I picture Robert standing in the living room, staring out of the window into his carefully considered garden, lettuce next to lettuce, cabbage next to cabbage. He strokes grey hair back from his forehead, soil beneath his nails. The older he gets, the more he begins to look like a child, despite the deep creases in his face, despite his dry skin – a child lost to my imagination for a long time, since he gave up on his plans – and I'm walking down the corridor at school when Robert appears before me, pushes a sweet into my mouth with a smile and points at a door, where a drawing is pinned up: mother, father, child. Big eyes, no mouths. A cleaning cloth in each hand.

NOTE

I open the door. I enter the bedroom of my childhood, but shrunken now, two metres by two metres. Inside is Nora. Our eyes meet and we start to laugh, mouths wrenched agape but soundless. Dust filters down, it coats our bodies, and we are falling, falling into a bright-lit room, a room I do not know.

'I think the sense of a self trapped in something is impossible to get over. That's the origin of all dualisms,' said Susan Sontag. And she also said that she believed all these binaries to be false: body or mind, thinking or feeling, imagination or reason.

Him or her, passion or constancy, living or lasting, dream or reality, children or freedom, mother or father, exception or standard, speech or silence, friendship or love, from here or from there, grateful or ungrateful, active or passive.

Szibilla

New born. New, not born. Would be nice. Still, at least I'm clean. Shame about the citrus oil. Washed off. Tampon in. I knew it. That menstrual cup is useless. Nora can have it back.

The next client is already waiting. Staring vacantly at a magazine. Waiting to lay herself, too, at Malita's feet. I walk alongside the pane of glass. The swimming pool is bright in the sun. Three people in it. Romi isn't one of them. The lift door opens with a *ding*. I enter. Faint judder. Second floor. Directly opposite the lift, my bedroom door. I slide the key into the lock. Step inside. Drape my bathrobe over the chair. Again, this nakedness. And my head switched off. Like at the end of the massage, when I tried to get back up. Lifting my upper body. Step one: sit up. Then the sudden feeling of wetness. My hand shot between my legs of its own accord. I pulled it back. Blood.

I put on my underwear, my sweatpants. The cami top, the shirt. Easy, easy. The one thought in my head had been this: I am at her mercy. But Malita's voice was utterly unconcerned.

'No big deal.'

I had already lain back down on my stomach. Malita pressed a towel into my hand. Warm. Tears well up. Embarrassing, all of this. That I couldn't even move. Or speak. Malita acting as though it happened to her clients every day.

'Shall I?'

My nod. Her dabbing at my upper thigh.

'Is that okay?' she asked.

More than okay. And terrible, awful. At her mercy! Malita simply stayed, dabbing. As if nothing on earth would disgust her. She asked me to turn over. Moving as if in slow motion, belly to back. Malita held out another towel. A fresh one. Would I prefer to do it myself? I shook my head. It was all I could do. She kept dabbing.

'Looks like we've knocked something loose in the last ninety minutes!' she said eventually. She dropped the towel into the sink. Passed me the robe. Everything seemed to be happening of its own accord. Removing the disposable underwear. Putting a fresh pair on. Bathrobe on top. Apologising. It was my first time, I said. With a menstrual cup. And she only said, 'Ah, those. You have to get used to them.' It was important to create a vacuum, she said, which wasn't easy at first. But no matter. Blood was nothing but water, protein and red blood cells. Then she focused on her list. A list of names?

My phone is on the desk, beside the textbook. No messages. Evidently Romi meant it when she said she wanted to spend the day alone. I pick up the book. *The Structure and Functions of the Human Body*. Walk back out of the room. Down the corridor. Not a soul in sight. Nor in what they call the hotel library. I'm glad. I slide the book onto the lone bookshelf. Ovaries, fallopian tubes, uterus, vagina. Between novels by Ken Follett and Nora Roberts. Still, there is at least a book about the Bödmeren Forest. And: *A General History of the Rhine Valley*. I can work with that. Distract myself from my embarrassment. From the fact that Nora still hasn't called. How powerful her absence. But there's no use thinking about it. It will be fine. As ever.

The only armchair in here is upholstered in black leather. I settle down into it, and it receives me with a sigh. How did I do it? I told Malita I wanted to thank her. Buy her lunch. She shook her head – she'd rather get a drink. She clocked off at one. Perhaps we could meet then? In the dining room? Just as a one-off. Not her usual practice.

Romi

Called Robert. 'Dad'. But it's not enough: I have to get him on the phone again, I have to speak to him, find the right questions. I imagine the telephone ringing.

Dad: *Yes?*

Me: *Looking back now, do you ever regret having the affair?*

D: ...

Me: *Or is it more that if it happened today you would decide sooner? You would choose your family before you were pressured into it?*

D: ...

Me: *Did 'deciding' always mean 'either/or'? For you, not just for Mum?*

D: ...

Me: *Have you ever consciously reflected on monogamy, on the history of it?*

D: ...

Me: *Do you think monogamy makes life easier?*

D: ...

Me: *Does/did it make it easier for you to love someone?*

D: ...

Me: *What does love mean to you, anyway?*

D: ...

Me: *Ever since you made that choice, it's seemed to me like you don't really love anything at all, despite what you claim.*

D: ...

Me: *If love means seeing another person the way they are, with all their flaws and in all their beauty, then I have to be honest with you: I don't feel as though you really see me. Or perhaps I'm wrong?*

D: ...

Me: You know, ever since that night in room 217, it feels like something has been growing inside me, growing out of me – not just a child but another component of my own ~~self~~ being.

D: ...

Me: Was it the same for you, with Tana?

D: ...

Me: I know you're not supposed to. I know you see it the same way as Szibilla: it's a stupid way to live, a stupid demand. This incessant hunger.

D: ...

Me: But you once felt that hunger too!

D: ...

Me: You honestly never considered leaving? Just walking out and never coming back?

D: ...

Me: Do you sometimes think back to the past, to the time before Tana, before Mum, even? Do you think about what you were like then, how you lived? What would your space have looked like if you could have arranged it entirely on your own terms?

D: ...

Me: Susan Sontag once said, 'An event that makes new feelings conscious is always the most important experience a person can have.' What do you think about that?

D: ...

Me: Have you experienced it too, the sort of struggle that fundamentally does you good, that entwines you more deeply with yourself and therefore with the world?

D: ...

Me: Am I working through something that concerns you too?

D: Put the pen away. There isn't any point.

Me: ...

D: ...

Me: I have sent myself into the labyrinth.

D: …

Me: *A labyrinth is a place where people get lost. And I want to lose myself, you know?*

D: …

Me: *To lose yourself means having to find yourself again.*

THE STORY OF ROBERT AND TANA (DANA? DIANA?)

He was married, with one child.
He started an affair with a woman from the same city.
His wife found out and made him choose: either family or affair.
He chose family.

THE STORY OF ROBERT AND TANA II

The man was married, with one child. He meditated regularly before a Celtic Tree Calendar, and one day he met a woman who sang her name on her answering machine and played a bodhrán in accompaniment. He spent hours on the phone with her, while in the living room his child planned dance shows and his wife played volleyball at the local gym, 800 metres from the school building where the family lived.

The child's mother was still a housewife at the time.

The voice of the woman on the phone had a rawness to it. Her hair was black and her bed was a wooden frame heaped with fir branches and covered in blankets. The bedding was pale beige, the woman's skin nearly white, and the man knew: he must not touch it, any of it, and yet he did.

THE STORY OF THE CHILD'S MOTHER

She had felt a jab somewhere to the right of her belly button, a hot needle boring into her skin, and she had excused herself and left the hall, showered in a hurry, dressed, and trudged the 800 metres home. The lights were on in the flat and there was no one in the living room, or in the main bedroom. In the second bedroom the child was sleeping on her belly, arms outstretched, and as the child's mother sat down on the toilet and the urine dripped into the bowl – slowly, because of the pain – she knew all at once where her husband was, although she couldn't really know at all. When, half an hour later, he quietly opened the front door and came to a sudden halt, he didn't really have to say anything.

Know or intuit, one or the other, heads or tails, day or night, lies or truth, faithful or unfaithful.

FIDELITY. *Some definitions according to the Oxford English Dictionary: 1.a. The quality of being faithful; faithfulness, loyalty, unswerving allegiance to a person, party, bond, etc. Const. to, towards. 1.c. Conjugal faithfulness. 1.e. Ecology. The degree of association of a species with a plant community.*

ROBERT

Going by the Celtic Tree Calendar, he was a hornbeam. 'Hornbeam, the tree of perseverance. A monument to loyalty.' This plant is characterised by a robust constitution, exceptionally hard wood, strong roots and dense-growing branches. Hornbeam is ideally suited for use in protective fences and borders. 'Hornbeam people go through life dauntlessly, ploughing a straight course.' They are difficult to throw off balance. They are characterised by constant industry and disciplined work. They provide support and protection to those around them.

THE CHILD

She is in the kitchen. The tap is dripping. She hears muffled voices. In the front room only the standing lamp is lit. A woman is on the sofa, her head thrown back, a sweep of dark hair across her glistening back. Two long legs poke out from underneath her body, bent at the knees, making of her a primeval creature. Robert's lips at her breast, and a rhythmic shudder rocks them both.

The next day, a hand. In it is a yellow ten-franc note. It sails down to the child's feet. Robert winks at her, a finger to his lips. The money is converted into gummy bears, which the child stuffs into her mouth. She says nothing to her mother.

A mouth full of sap, I swallow. I am a tree, I am loyal, like Robert, the hornbeam; I persevere. Who does not?

SILVIA

The child's mother said: Don't ever lie to me again.
He lied to her.
He met the woman with the bodhrán many times.
On one morning in August, almost a year after she had discovered the affair, the child's mother woke up to her husband sleeping next to her, totally relaxed, one eyelid twitching now and then. She shook him awake, and she said: It's time to decide. Otherwise you have to leave.
He decided.

DECIDE, *verb. To resolve, to choose, determine or settle, etymologically derived from the Latin dēcīdere, infinitive of dēcīdō ('cut off, decide'), from dē ('down from') + caedō ('cut').*

THE TREE CALENDAR

- *Love is a sore subject for hornbeams.*
- *They protect and deeply care for their partners.*
- *This can, however, feel oppressive and controlling.*

If the Tree Calendar didn't operate by date of birth, if Robert had been able to choose freely, he would have chosen to be a sycamore, wouldn't he? Sycamore people are lovers of freedom. Of evolution and unfolding. They never hesitate for long. They refuse the confines of pattern, including predetermined models of behaviour. Independence is important to them.

Yet: A sycamore is what I am! (At least, if I go by my birthday.) Although, isn't Nora more of a sycamore really? While I am a fir.
- *Fir people know exactly what they want.*
- *They are afraid of being hurt.*

- *They put up protective walls and retreat when things get too emotional for them.*
- *They are immensely delicate, sensitive people, though on the outside they can appear cold.*

ROBERT II

In the beginning he would lay the breakfast table at weekends. He'd fold the napkins into birds – first doves, then swans, then penguins – and boil eggs, eight minutes exactly, just as Silvia liked them.

He reorganised the living room, cleared out unwanted books, bought Silvia the grass-green armchair she'd long been hankering after and positioned it in the middle of the room, a little towards the window. When Silvia sat down in it for the first time, she smiled, but she never rested in it longer than it took to skim a newspaper.

Little by little, Robert lost his colour. The lines around his eyes and on his forehead grew more rutted, his beard pricked Silvia when they kissed. They were kissing again, in those first months, but only rarely after that. They lost sight of each other. When their eyes did meet, observing one another in the mornings, it was only fleetingly, wearily, through the steam that rose from their coffee.

Robert stopped doing yoga. He stopped walking for hours in the forest. He stopped going to the gym. Cooking, reading. Yet he continued to meditate. And he kept the school building scoured and clean, with abrasive disinfectants that burned his hands, because he was no longer wearing plastic gloves. His voice was beginning to sound strange.

FAILURE. *Some definitions according to the OED: 1.a. A failing to occur, be performed, or be produced; 3.a. The fact of failing to effect one's purpose; want of success; 3.b. A thing or person that proves unsuccessful.*

SILVIA II

She started training as a teacher, leaving the house for the college in the mornings, and when she returned, she was busy studying, preparing, sometimes finding time to see her friends.

THE CHILD II

At lunchtime the child made pizza with Robert, or they cooked spaghetti with ketchup. Every now and then, Robert would bring out two bottles of Orangina. That was a good omen. They clinked bottles and Robert told her stories about the numerous Swiss Alpine passes: Bernina, Julier, Klausen; or about the region of Albula, which as a boy he had crossed every summer on his bike, to spend two weeks in the high Alpine valley of the Engadin, staying in a simple mountain cabin with his whole family: father, mother, children. But no matter how much he talked or how hard the child tried to tell equally wonderful stories in return, spirit-lifting, funny stories, it brought no gleam back to Robert. The grey remained.

THE CHILD III

In the afternoons, when the child was alone in the flat after school, she went into the living room to watch talk shows and TV series.

When her parents were home, she sat in her bedroom, writing individual words on paper and eavesdropping. But she heard only doors, opening and being closed again. Her parents did not fight and barely spoke.

THE CHILD IV

Only as a teenager did the child begin to speak more freely, when she found her first real friend. When she found Nora. Nora, who liked to speak just as much, and often; until recently.

(12:51. I really should have some proper food.)

Szibilla

Yes, it was her. Romi. Slinking into the dining room. Intent on going unseen. Not seeing me, either. Eyes trained straight ahead. A meagre helping of food on the tiniest plate. Then she is gone. And I am left alone with Madame Ibuprofen. One more, I think. I squeeze the last drops of juice out of the wedge of lemon. Let it drip into my glass of water. Then I take a sip and wash the tablet down. The Botticelli painting on the wall. Venus looks altogether less relaxed than the *Large Reclining Woman with Parrot* above my sofa. A gift from Nora. A perfect present for my thirty-fourth, she said. And the woman in the poster looked like me, she added. In a good way.

She too is blonde. She possesses wide, strong thighs. She wears a petticoat, lying outstretched, eyes closed. Her head rests on her arm, one languid hand in her hair. At the far left, by her head: the green parrot. A faithful comrade. Lucky for some. Would be nice to have the woman's nonchalance as well. Had she bought me that too, I asked Nora. She gave me a wink. Took a bottle of Zinfandel out of her rucksack.

'It was sold out,' she said. 'But I found this, and I've already ordered the petticoat. I'll give it to you for Christmas.'

She headed off towards the kitchen. I examined the petticoat more closely. Yellow. It ended underneath her bare breasts. The breasts seemed to be looking. I called after Nora that she should save her money. And her: 'No expense spared for you, Sib!' In a moment she was back with the glasses. How easy she makes things for me. No doubt it would be easier today. If she were here.

Here is Malita. Strolling at a leisurely pace through the dining room. The expansive motion of her hips. It's as though she savours every step. She sits down across from me. Nods. Friendly, but aloof. Maybe she thinks I'm a weirdo after all.

'Are you full?' she asks.

'I'm stuffed,' I say. 'And you, you're not hungry? After such a long morning!'

She smiles and waves a dismissive hand. 'Oh, it's only lunchtime. I'll have a black tea.'

I order us one each. Examine Malita. Her straight brows, filled in with pencil. Around her eyes: the most delicate of lines, visible only at certain moments. The lower ones when she smiles. The upper, now, as she looks around the dining room. She must be older than I am. Forty or so, perhaps. Already the waiter is setting down a cup on the table, one in front of each of us. Malita reaches into her bag.

'Would you like some too?' she asks, pointing surreptitiously at a hip flask. She pours us both a liberal splash.

'I recommend a helping of rum every day. Lunchtime is perfect, actually. Then a quick power nap, and you're back up and running,' she says. She slips the flask back into her bag. 'Are you here on your own?'

I shake my head. 'It's a bit complicated.'

'Let me guess,' Malita says. 'You're here with your prepubescent child? Or with your ex? With your soon-to-be-ex? With your arch-rival? With your grandmother?'

'With an acquaintance.'

'And what's complicated about that?'

'The circumstances. Also, we're night and day.'

'So why are you on holiday together?'

'It just sort of happened that way.'

'How?'

'Let's be honest. Would you want to go on holiday here?' I ask.

Malita thinks. Then she says, 'If I had the money, I wouldn't go on holiday to some dingy old spa hotel like this, I'd go to a proper one. One with a glossy floor instead of old-fashioned carpets. With a spa three times the size. But that's only in my dreams – awake, I'm here.'

'What's the pay like in your line of work? Bad? Or really bad?'

'It's alright. But I won't be buying a house any time soon.' She hesitates. Then she says, 'My mother lives with me. That's *my* complicated story. Not appropriate for a tea-and-rum lunch-break. Cheers!'

'To the complexities of life,' I say.

We clink cups. Malita drinks quickly. The temperature of her tea doesn't seem to bother her. She has three more backs to see to this afternoon, she tells me. Would I like to come for a walk down to the village afterwards? Maybe play some pool?

'Are you night or day, by the way?' she asks, without waiting for me to answer the first question.

'I'm sorry?'

'You said that you and your acquaintance – your friend? – are like night and day.'

'I'm night,' I answer promptly.

'Ah. So those blonde curls are your disguise.'

I don't need one, I say. A disguise.

And her: 'We all need a disguise.'

'Where shall we meet?' I ask.

'Outside the hotel, just after six.'

'Perfect. We can jailbreak for a bit.'

'Exactly.'

Malita glances at her watch. Time for her power nap, she says. Before the next client turns up.

I watch her go. Is this the same person who wiped away my blood this morning? Again, that brief rigidity. Then I take out my phone.

Hi Romi. I'm out the rest of the day. Exploring the valley. Text me if you hear anything.

I take another sip of tea. The giant enters the dining room. Behind him is the Magic Flute woman. Now the teenage girl. Headphones over her ears. She sits down with her parents and immediately opens a comic book.

I google *rhine valley museum, rhine valley market, rhine valley sightseeing*. I've got to find something eventually.

Romi

THE STORY OF ROBERT AND TANA III

IT COULD HAVE GONE LIKE THIS

The man chose the woman with the black hair. He spent many hours in her wooded bed. She caressed him awake and caressed him to sleep, she sang to him, and he bloomed, his face growing full and young. He left everything behind him: the child and the child's mother, the schoolhouse, the schoolhouse corridors. There was only him and the woman with the black hair, and the various objects that presented themselves to him for observation: the leaves on the sycamore tree, the hornbeams by the verge, the snail on the pavement, which he took carefully into his palm and carried into the forest, placing it in the undergrowth; and he simply kept on going, through the forest and beyond, and he travelled to the places where both of them were drawn, the Rhine Valley, the Forest of Bregenz, Vienna.

And yet the longing would perhaps have remained.

And daily life would have set in.

The woman with the black hair doesn't like the way he drinks his coffee on the balcony in the morning. She doesn't like coffee at all.

He doesn't like how she spits when she talks. And sometimes she looks as though she isn't quite right in the head, but when he brings it up she won't acknowledge it.

But he doesn't throw any knives, the way he did with the mother of his child, not into the sink and not onto the floor. He puts the knife next to his bread, still with a little butter on it, he takes a deep breath then goes outside for a moment, gets some fresh air.

Every now and then, the woman with the black hair uses a perfume he cannot smell.

Sometimes he wants to be alone. She doesn't.

She sometimes wants to rent a yurt and spend the night in it. He doesn't.

But there is still something that glitters between them. She still likes sex with him and he with her, and when they are in each other's arms, it is better than anything they have known in all their lives. There is something vast and simple in it: safety.

IT COULD HAVE GONE LIKE THIS II

He had left everything behind. He had gone wherever the mood took him, travelling with the woman with the black hair. Always overland, or where necessary by boat; they were in perpetual motion, rarely staying more than one night in the same place.

One day they were sitting on a cliff in Japan, gazing out across the dark blue sea. And all at once he remembered his child. The mother of his child. The schoolhouse, the corridor, the Celtic Tree Calendar pinned to the wall. And suddenly he missed his child and his old life so much it felt as though his chest was being torn apart. Suddenly he couldn't move his legs, they were as heavy as though filled with sap. The woman with the black hair heaved him over her shoulders, she carried him downhill to the next train station. They went to Tokyo, to the airport, and travelled back to the city where he had lived, and at first glance everything was just as he remembered. The square outside the school building. The swings, the climbing frame, his child playing with a boomerang on the lawn; the boomerang always returned to her, no matter the slant at which she threw it. The child had grown – she was half a head taller at least – and her hair was longer too, down to her shoulders. There was a new expression on her face. Something austere and tranquil that the man did not notice until he stood before the child and threw his arms out wide. She looked at him round-eyed, mouth closed. She had no idea who he was.

IT COULD HAVE GONE LIKE THIS III

He didn't want to go back. He didn't know what that would even mean, because he didn't know where he had come from. His previous life was like writing on a blackboard, wiped over with a damp sponge: what remained was an evaporating mark, growing smaller second by second, until only a smudge of chalk dust was left on the board.

SILVIA III

IT COULD HAVE GONE LIKE THIS

Silvia took the decision herself. She left her husband, left the school building and moved to another city; the child wanted to go with her. While Silvia studied for her teacher's exams at one end of the table, the child studied for her school exams at the other. They passed the jug of water back and forth – they were a household of women, and they stayed that way: mother, daughter.

IT COULD HAVE GONE LIKE THIS II

Silvia took the decision herself. She left her husband, left the school building and found a small flat for herself and the child in the same city, with a parquet floor and big windows. On the weekends, the mother's new boyfriend came to visit: Saturday morning at 9 a.m. sharp he would be on the doorstep, a rustling bag of fresh croissants in his grasp. At first, all he left at the flat were those bags, but then a jumper, then his jogging shoes, then a whole suitcase. The new boyfriend took up more and more room in Silvia's life and the life of her child – the child's father, meanwhile, less and less. He only phoned the child once a year, on her birthday.

IT COULD HAVE GONE LIKE THIS III

Silvia and Robert took a mutual decision to separate. They all left the school behind them and went streaming off in different directions: Silvia found a flat in the west of the city, Robert in the east, and the child shuttled back and forth. She had two bedrooms, one in the west and one in the east. Two rooms just for her. And two parents who talked about the days behind them and the days to come. Good times. Not a time of struggle, anyway, even if struggle had seemed likely, since the child was already on the verge of transition: from girl to woman. Her body had begun to pinch, like a pair of too-small shoes.

IT COULD HAVE GONE LIKE THIS IV

Silvia took the decision herself. She found a flat and enrolled at the university to study French, took courses on French symbolism, on Simone de Beauvoir, and visited the great French cities four times a year. After three years, she and the child moved to Lyon; Silvia opened a little café and greeted every customer with a firm handshake. She looked them in the eye when they spoke, and Silvia always spoke to her customers; and when they left the café there was a warmth in their bellies, in part from the tea they had been served but above all because they had been seen.

IT COULD HAVE GONE LIKE THIS V

Silvia took the decision herself. She left her husband, left the school building and her child. She left everything behind her. She shed the role of wife and mother like an old skin.

IT WENT LIKE THIS

After three years, Silvia finished training to be a primary school teacher. Three years in which she carried her studies like a protective shield, filling every spare second with preparation and background reading; three years in which anything that was not scheduled received only the scantest attention.

Three years in which the child grew four inches in height and eyed herself sceptically in the mirror every morning: the broadening hips, the rounder belly, the body as a whole, which now seemed incapable of binding anything together, not what was inside it or anything around it either.

Three years in which Robert did little more than three things: cleaning the school, meditating, roaring down mountain passes on his motorbike. And drinking Orangina with the child.

IT WENT LIKE THIS II

Robert took Silvia away on holiday to celebrate getting her diploma. They brought the child – who was now a teenager – along as well. The teenager couldn't believe her eyes. The way Robert put his arm around Silvia, and she let him. The way Silvia bent towards him and kissed a smear of sauce away from the corner of his mouth. The way Robert ordered three glasses of wine and let the teenager have one too. Said they were toasting 'to us'.

The teenager was sure it was a passing phase.

But it wasn't.

The two of them stayed together.

The three of them stayed together, but they never talked about the silence and the stillness that had preceded what her parents called happiness. All of it was swept under the rug, a family heirloom, heavy and cumbersome. How many fathers and mothers had trodden on it, how many children had lain on it, on the griefs, the unspoken words of the generations gone before.

NORA

IT WENT LIKE THIS

Once, Nora too lay on a carpet much like mine, her family's carpet. She too ran her fingers over the patterns, until she – like I – realised she had legs and stood on them and began to walk around, small circles only, which grew bigger and bigger. The carpet was still there – hers and mine – but neither of us noticed it any more: habit had made a blind spot of it.

IT COULD HAVE BEEN LIKE THIS

Nora had never told anyone, but she regretted having a baby. Becoming a mother. Not finishing any of the courses she had begun. One morning she startled awake to find that panic was rising in her throat. All at once it dawned on her the opportunities she might have had: she could have chosen not to have the baby and to finish her psychology degree. Or no, to do an apprenticeship after all. Or to complete a three-month course in programming in Stockholm, then get a job. Or to go travelling for years on end, taking casual work to earn the roof over her head and the food in her stomach.

It would still be possible, all of it: she could leave everything behind. This city. This flat. This child on the playmat at her feet. She went to the door and reached for the handle. At that moment she glanced back over her shoulder and saw the baby holding out its little arms towards her.

IT COULD HAVE BEEN LIKE THIS

Nora lay back down beside the child. She was at a loss. Her breathing quickened. Sleep, she thought, she had to sleep. And she hoped that while she slept, all of it would subside, all of it would fall away, and the old skin would simply shed itself.

THE WAY IT IS

Meret is lying on Nora's carpet, the family heirloom, and Leon on mine. Soon the baby will be too.

The duvet cover is sticking to my skin. I sit up, pulling the fabric taut. The lunch plate, still lying on the bed, begins to slide, moving in the direction of the floor; I grab it, put it on the bedside table with the fork.

I can hear Nora as though she were here in the room with me, although in fact it was very early on, when I had known Dennis barely two weeks, that she asked me, 'Are you using Dennis as a way to avoid things, because you've got yourself into a situation that feels too cramped, with a second kid and a flat out in the countryside?'

'No,' I said, 'that's not it. I wasn't unhappy before I met Dennis.'

And Nora said, 'You weren't unhappy with Vural, either, when you met Phil. Right? But you still broke up with him.'

I said that was different.

'Because you didn't have any kids, you and Vural?'

I stayed quiet, and Nora went on. 'Your life is still very much enmeshed with Phil's.'

'Yeah, and I want it to be,' I said, to which Nora replied, 'Guess we'll see, won't we?' and then, after a short pause, 'What's he like, anyway, this Dennis guy?'

Anni

There's a tremendous thud and clatter coming from Nora's room, then on the stairs, and then suddenly she is standing in the kitchen. I grip Meret a little more tightly in my arms.

'Nora!'

She hasn't even bothered to put on a pair of trousers. She's still so slim. So young! Meret begins to cry.

'Love! How are you feeling?' I ask.

'Can I have something to eat?'

'Yes, of course!'

I stand up, still holding Meret close. 'What do you fancy?'

She's already helping herself from the cupboard.

'Would you like to sit down?' I ask.

Suddenly Meret is screaming so loudly that I don't catch Nora's reply. She might not have said anything at all. She turns to us, not really looking at me, only Meret. Such a blurred gaze. She takes the child from my arms and leaves, carrying a plate of sausage and bread. Upstairs, the door slams shut. The tap is dripping. I shut it off a little more tightly.

The tomatoes on the windowsill are warm. I'll put them in a nice quiche. The recipe is in the bread bin. No, in the rack next to the oven. Why are my hands trembling like this? Ah, here it is. Then I'll tidy up some of my things in the bathroom so that Nora can spread out a bit. We could drive down to the village and get her some make-up. A body lotion, a revitalising shower gel. Wait, no, it's Sunday. Perhaps I've already got something she might like. My clay and hibiscus shower gel, maybe. Maybe then she'll talk to me. Is that too much to ask?

The knife glides through the tomatoes. I should wait a little longer. I have things to do.

Romi

I close the notebook. My phone is still beside the bed. As I reach for it, the mattress flexes and the springs give a dull squeak; I switch on my phone: one message from Szibilla. Nothing else.

If Nora asked me again today, I would tell her that Dennis and I met at a networking event at the txt-akademie, that I arrived much too late, having been delayed between St Gallen and Zurich by a death on the tracks. At last I found myself in the lobby, a newspaper under my arm, watching the other visitors stream purposefully along the broad hall.

I felt like turning around, but instead I shook myself and headed for the café in the foyer, taking up position at the bar. I didn't notice the man next to me until he spoke. Why was I reading that liberal rag, he asked me, pointing at the newspaper. I eyed him: his stubbly beard, his hair tousled in all directions, and the dark eyes at rest underneath, an attentive gaze. Someone had left it on the train, I said. I used to read it when I was a student, because my flatmate at the time had a subscription.

He asked what I'd studied, and I said German with a focus on philosophy, and that I'd interned at a publishing house between my bachelor's and master's, in editorial, and that now, as a freelancer, I felt somewhat at sea.

'So that's why you're here now?' he asked. 'To find your sea legs?'

'You could put it like that, yes,' I said, taken aback by his clear, bright voice, a voice for audiobooks – he could read *The*

Wall with that voice, I told him, the Marlen Haushofer novel, and he laughed.

'*The Wall*?'

And I said: 'Just as an example.'

I went on to say that I was looking for opportunities to transition back into publishing, but it was tricky to establish myself in the business, even trickier than I'd thought. Maybe it was time I looked for a simpler job and just wrote on the side – that was what I'd always wanted, to write, but I'd never really dared.

'An even trickier business, that,' he said, adding that he was a writer himself, of poetry.

I asked what brought him here.

He had met up with an old friend for coffee, he answered, and now he fancied another. 'Do you want one as well?' he asked, and introduced himself: Dennis.

I nodded and sat down on the barstool beside him.

Speaking of establishing oneself here, he said – emphasising 'here' and 'establishing' – he had just come back the night before from Athens, where his mother had grown up. He used to visit several times a year, but less and less these days, for various reasons. And today, in particular, there was a certain feeling he couldn't shake – a vague sense of being neither 'from there' nor 'from here', not 'established', in inverted commas. Did I know what he meant?

'Who, in your opinion, is "from here"?' I asked, turning the paper around and pointing to a picture of Christoph Blocher with his index finger raised. The headline next to it declared that the nationalists were set to remain the most popular party in Switzerland at the upcoming elections.

'I'm just saying that I'm tired of it, today, fiddling around with this puzzle again,' Dennis said, and he put his hand on the newspaper, covering the photograph of Blocher. 'And as always the pieces don't quite fit together. They don't make a proper picture, just a patchwork. Sometimes I feel like hurling myself against the wall, see if I can break through it at last. So you may be right about Marlen Haushofer. Anyway. Apologies if I'm rambling at you.'

I said that at least his patchwork was based on something concrete, unlike mine, and that I didn't mind the rambling.

He asked what I meant.

'My parents call themselves Swiss, I call myself Swiss. I fall into certain categories: white, hetero, middle-class. Yet there's more about this country that feels foreign to me than familiar. What am I supposed to attribute that to? Specifically?'

He hesitated, holding my gaze for a long time, more directly than almost anybody ever has. I felt something course through me, top to bottom, and he said, 'Because of Greece and all that stuff – yeah, it's a way of making it easier for myself, of course. But fundamentally I'm almost as white and middle-class as you are. Unlike my mother, back in the day.'

'When did she come here?' I asked.

'In the seventies.'

'Slap bang into the heyday of right-wing populism, then.'

'Yeah. From a military dictatorship to a Switzerland that was considering turfing out all its "excess immigrants". It was tough.'

I asked why she had chosen Switzerland, of all places.

'Because of my dad,' Dennis said. He told me that his mother had always believed that this country was in all respects progressive. She was surprised to find that working mothers were referred to as neglectful, and that many ordinary citizens – and the political system as a whole – were hostile to foreigners. When they were home alone, his mother had only spoken to him in Greek.

Dennis pointed at my bag and asked, 'And you? Are you the stereotype of the hard-working Swiss citizen?'

'I was brought up on all that stuff,' I said. 'Work, work, be useful. I'm a clock that winds itself up overnight.'

A wicked smile flashed across Dennis's face, then he said, 'This country isn't neutral, it's twisted. Speaking for myself, one thing I don't like is the requirement to endlessly plan absolutely everything all the time. To endlessly perform and prove everything. Where are the gaps? The leisure, really.'

He crossed his legs and stretched his slender upper body, and his mustard-yellow jumper pulled taut and slipped upwards.

'I'm wallowing in it right now, as it happens. Leisure. I need an overdose. Helps you to self-regulate naturally – it's the same thing with sugar.'

'The greatest luxury of all.'

'Sugar or leisure?'

'Both,' I said. 'But if you overdose on sugar, all that happens is that sooner or later you'll be spending more time at the doctor's. If you overdose on leisure, you'd better hope you have a Swiss passport. Otherwise you'll be out on your ear.'

We chatted briefly about the Swiss People's Party's election poster, which depicted a white sheep kicking a black sheep off the Swiss flag, and Dennis listed for me some of the insults that had come his way: 'wop', 'Islamist', 'weren't all the Ancient Greeks a bunch of poofs?' Still, he said, he had to admit: he was currently enjoying lapping up the kind of sugary leisure that was denied to the privileged.

'Where?' I asked. Dennis said he'd been living for a while in St Gallen, and that although the city didn't interest him much, it did allow him a certain freedom to fluctuate, a state of temporariness. He knew no one, owed nothing to anyone but himself, and two or three times a week he would dole out lunch at the soup kitchen. He quite liked East Switzerland, in fact, especially the Alpstein mountains, which he had hiked last autumn. He had been impressed by the way the ground fell away on either side of the mountain ridge, then swept back up on the other side towards the next peak, giving the impression that the region was higher and more extensive than it actually was — it was a mini mountain range, really. I said I was living there too. St Gallen, for the time being.

'What a coincidence,' he said.

He was surveying the bottles behind the bar, and yet his enthusiasm rubbed off on me as he described hiking in Greece — it was better there than I was picturing, he said. I was probably thinking of the sea, of the summer heat, the tavernas packed with tourists, or the Acropolis. But in autumn and in winter it was astonishing how surly the Greek landscape could become, the way the wind would whip up out of nowhere and roil the sea into high waves.

There were, he continued, outstanding opportunities for hiking. In the Peloponnese he especially liked the Taygetus mountains and Profitis Ilias, the highest peak, where a tiny chapel was perched at the top. Its roof was in a state of disrepair, but the bells recessed into its stony sides chimed in the wind as you gazed out across the sea into the distance, and all of it was far away from the camp at Moria; and yes, indeed, there were a lot of refugees, on Lesbos but also the Aegean islands more generally, including at the northern border. The aid workers were overwhelmed, and they weren't the only ones, whereas in Switzerland—

I sit up in bed and rub my face, fingers pressing into my eye sockets. It's dark now, like it was in Nora's room yesterday.

'So how come this was more than just a one-night stand?' I hear her ask.

I take my hands away, see points of light dancing on the grey bedclothes, fading one by one. I open my notebook. The pencil scratches across the paper.

NOTE

Nora: *Why don't you get to the point?*

Me: ...

N: *Come on, tell me, what is it about him, this Dennis guy?*

Me: ...

N: *You're taking this risk – a significant risk – because of him!*

Me: *I know. And yes, there are other things I could tell you about him, about how we met and what he means to me. But I could never tell you everything, I could never fully express it all, because the most essential things defy words, always.*

N: *So you're trying to preserve it, keep it some big romantic secret.*

Me: *No.*

N: *Then why not tell me?*

Me: ...

N: *Look, you're the one who was so desperate to talk!*

Me: *Yes. But to speak is to search. To search for meaning, for connections. So is writing, too.*

N: ...

Me: *What I want, when I speak and when I write, is to cast off my skin, to shed it layer by layer. I want to peel words from their shells and discover that many things go deeper and are greater than I first thought. And if speaking – or language – shapes my thinking, then I expand if my language expands, and my thinking expands too. And so do my emotions.*

N: ...

Me: *Maybe that's the reason why I don't understand your silence, Nora. Or rather, it's why I can't stand it. Because it feels so much like a stalemate.*

N: ...

Dennis and I lingered in the café for a long time, and I talked a lot. It felt unconstrained and easy, which is a rare experience for me. I told him about my degree, my flatshare, my job as a speech-to-text reporter; about Leon's birth and how afterwards I had begun a search I still couldn't put a name to. And Dennis told me about studying in Vienna and returning to Switzerland. He told me about meeting his ex-wife and working as a dramaturg on the independent theatre circuit, his transfer to a theatre company, which didn't satisfy him in the way he'd hoped. Inwardly he had felt torn: the responsibilities on all sides, the endless picking over every idea. And he told me, also, how long he'd spent trying to talk himself round: *this is what you always wanted.* Yet more and more, he began to wonder, Why aren't I happy now? He told me how, suddenly, every day was tougher than the last, as though each morning he woke up with the soles of his shoes covered in a layer of glue that wouldn't dry, making every step an effort. It wasn't just the job that wasn't right, it was his relationship and everything that went with it. At long last, he chose. He left everything behind him: his job, his wife, the chic flat that belonged to her, their mutual friends and acquaintances, almost all of whom he knew through her, and he left the security his wife had given him all those years, not least of the financial kind. Now he was eking out the money he had put aside, living frugally and trying to write, not putting too much pressure on himself or too little, hoping to publish in the foreseeable future, and this time perhaps a little more successfully than on his first attempt. He ought to be happy, he said, to be free at last; but, well, it had come a little late, the transformation, at forty-one – although of course it was never too late to start again.

'Is it really starting again? Isn't it more like another step in the process?' I asked.

He nodded and explained that most people didn't see it that way. That sometimes he even doubted it himself, when he woke up early and alone, and remembered that he'd once had everything he'd ever wanted, or so it seemed. That other people, even friends, said, 'You've gone back a step. At least one.' Or, as his mother put it: 'It's a pity to lose those years.'

'And she may be right,' he said at last. 'That they were lost years.'

'What did you lose?' I asked.

'I could be somewhere else right now,' Dennis said. 'If I'd got out sooner.'

And I sensed a heaviness that drew him suddenly smaller.

'Well, anyway,' he said, pulling himself up straight again, 'I'm certainly feeling a bit out of place in *here*.' He looked around him.

'Same,' I replied, adding, 'from here, from there.' And then we stood up as if by agreement, left the building quietly and walked in the direction of the lake. A strong wind blew, and we turned our collars up as high as they would go, and while I observed Dennis in profile, the intent face, the watchful eyes, I realised how comfortable I felt with him, in this common rhythm, not too fast, not too slow, simply walking, and I never wanted to stop.

'It's amazing, really, this place where we live,' Dennis said as we reached Sechseläutenplatz. The opera house in the background looked very small compared to the vast square in front of it, paved in immaculately shaped, shimmering, silvery-grey quartzite. 'In the stronghold of capitalism,' I said as we crossed the square, adding how glad I was that there were so many things I didn't have to worry about – food, education, a roof over my head – but also how depressing I found it too, how badly I wanted to strip away some of this splendour, this luxury that could only be had at the expense of so many others.

Dennis nodded; we had reached the lake. A woman and a child were throwing nut-sized pieces of bread into the water, the ducks lunging at them greedily.

'If it had been up to you,' I asked, 'would you rather have grown up in Greece?'

'Tough question.'

The child hit one of the ducks on the head, and it started quacking loudly.

'We were born into a particular time, a particular country, without being given a choice,' I said. 'We absorbed its customs, its sights. We've internalised so much of that. Sometimes it seems almost impossible to liberate myself from that.'

'But you're thinking about yourself so passively,' Dennis said, and I replied, 'Sometimes I can't help it,' – and he touched my little finger. 'Same,' he said. That was all, just that touch, that word, spreading and heating up everything inside me. At seven o'clock at the train station, we parted. He had to go back to St Gallen, he said, and I'd booked myself a room at a no-frills hotel in the neighbourhood of Oerlikon, my little city break, a Christmas present from Nora.

NOTE

(WHAT I CAN SAY, NORA.)

I am a house of many rooms. One of the largest of these had been filled for many years with faded furniture. The wallpaper brittle, the floor scuffed, a thick carpet in one corner, and everywhere the dust. I stepped inside this room many times: my eye would fall on the drawn curtains, and I would be paralysed.

One day, abruptly, I found I could move. I pushed the rocking chair against the wall and the barstool into the corner, gathered up the bits of dust into my hands as best I could, opened the mottled window, and let them drift off into the night. And when I turned around, Dennis was stumbling into the room.

He sat down on the floor. In one movement I tore a broad strip of paper off the wall, revealing the bright plasterboard beneath. Dennis waited until I was sitting next to him, and together we gazed at the plaster and projected what we saw.

'Water,' he said. 'It's flowing very quickly. I dive down, I see the world flipped on its head. Are those clouds there at the bottom, by the riverbed?'

'A forest,' I said, 'I'm walking through it. Birds are startled into flight, their beating wings a sign that tells me where you are.'

'Knock knock,' he said. 'So this is where you've been waiting all this time. Waiting for me?'

LEISURE: *Opportunity afforded by freedom from occupations. The state of having time at one's own disposal; time which one can spend as one pleases; free or unoccupied time. From Old French* leisir, *representing Latin* licēre, *to be permitted.*

Dennis was lying in room 217, limbs outstretched. His naked body made a hollow in the mattress. He said, 'The prophet Elias was a sailor. One day he decided to live in a place where the people knew nothing of the sea. He put his oar under his arm and asked the first person he saw, "What is this I'm carrying?" The answer came: "An oar." The next person he met gave him the same reply: "That is an oar." Elias walked far enough and high enough uphill that at last he met a shepherd who stared at him confused and said, "What that is I cannot tell you." At this highest point, Elias built his house. From there the sea was a single shimmer, an endless carpet of light.'

I lay down next to Dennis, eyes on the wooden ceiling, and asked, 'Why did Elias want to leave his boat?'

'Being a sailor was a dangerous job. He didn't want to die before his time,' Dennis said. 'But most of all he wanted to see the water in a new way.'

'He wouldn't have preferred to fly?'

'He didn't know what flying was.'

'Not even from his dreams?'

'Not even that.'

He paused. Then he asked, 'Will you come with me to Greece this summer?'

'Yes,' I said without stopping to think, and I turned to Dennis and pulled him towards me.

He studied me as though I'd appeared out of nowhere; I felt naked, unpleasantly so, and thought about pulling the covers over me, but I let it be, I simply lay there — wan and formless.

Nora: Is that all you can tell me?
Me: Isn't that already quite a lot?

Anni

I knock. Silence. I knock harder. Has she gone deaf, on top of everything else? No, now I hear something, it's coming from just the other side of the door. It opens with a jerk.

'What is it?' Nora asks. Her hair is a mess.

I wipe my hands on my apron. As long as I don't lose my temper.

'Is there anything I can do for you?' I ask.

Nora says nothing.

'I just wondered – I've been thinking. Maybe you'd fancy a trip to the hairdresser's? I could do with a cut and colour myself. I'm sure Dorothe could find time for us tomorrow.'

Still, Nora says nothing. She has put on a pair of shorts. They gape at the waist.

'There's still some tomato quiche left if you're hungry,' I say.

There, something in her face just changed – didn't it? She shakes her head.

Meret is in the corner, staring at the wall. Strange. I lean forward slightly. I'm too far away to see what's in the bin. Some sort of packaging? Nora is looking at me searchingly.

'Shall I take the little one downstairs for a bit?' I ask.

Nora hesitates. Then she nods.

'Are you coming, Meret?' I ask.

She doesn't move a millimetre. Nora kneels down beside her, and the girl turns to her mother and nuzzles her head into her shoulder. If only she'd do that with me. Nora picks her up and presses her into my arms. A short-lived whimper, then the child is calm. Meret weighs heavy in my embrace.

'Don't worry,' I say to Nora.

The bedroom door is already closed, and I am standing in the hall with Meret.

Romi

Six forty-four in the evening; how time flies, and I'm still in this room with the one window, the one wardrobe, the little table. The carpet swims before my eyes, blending contourlessly into the white wall, the wooden ceiling. The longer I lie here, the harder it is for me to breathe, the more impossible the thought of going out. Where would I go? Nothing from Nora. Is she still in bed, motionless and silent? I see her in my mind's eye, facing me, a soap bubble floating above her. The bubble bursts, soaking Nora's hair; red spills out over her, over the floor, and now the walls are red as well.

'He's good in bed though, Dennis, right?' she had said before, after I'd told her barely anything about him, even though I'd known him for two weeks by then.

And I said, my voice a rattle in my memory, the syllables drawn out: 'I'd say Dennis and I are extremely well suited, in a certain way. Not just sexually.'

Nora smiled to herself, said, 'Sure, but it hasn't been very long. I thought the same thing about Emrik, thanks to the hormones. It started off all lovey-dovey. But you of all people, Romi, should know how quickly that can change.'

Six forty-five. An email pings in, a newsletter about the Women's Strike. On 14 June we are taking to the streets.

'For us!' Nora has been saying since January, when the committee was formed. 'I'm organising it for us! And for our children!'

I have lost my way, got myself on the wrong track somehow; I have too much to lose. I need to concentrate. I pull up Phil's profile. Call his number. It rings four times, then he picks up.

'Phil!' I say.

'Yeah? What's up?'

'How are you two getting on?'

'We're in the middle of dinner. Is it important?'

'I miss you guys.'

'Can we talk later?'

'Okay.'

'I'll give you a call once Leon is asleep.'

'Give him a kiss from me.'

Szibilla

Malita's firm tread coming up the stairs. Eddy's Bar. She waves, two beers. Or would you rather wine? Wine, okay. The gloomy ambience. Flyers advertising local events. She picks up the glasses. I point to a tall table at the back of the room. Malita nods in the direction of one at the front. We mutely agree to one in the middle.

'So this is the place to be, eh?' I ask.

Malita nods. Puts the glasses down. She needs a drink every now and then, she says. An evening spent among other people. She glances around. A young couple at the pool table. Two men at the bar, their backs to us. An old dartboard hanging crooked on the wall behind her.

'It's not usually this empty,' she says. 'Bank holiday, and suddenly everybody makes themselves scarce. So where do you live, then?'

'Zurich,' I say. 'Well, just outside it.'

She raises her eyebrows. 'Oh really, the Swiss Gold Coast? But I don't see your Armani jacket?'

'All I'll say is this: Bülach!'

'Wow,' Malita says. 'How did you pull that off?'

'Have you ever been there?'

'No,' she says. 'But it can't be as bad as I thought if *you* live there. As long as they haven't built that nuclear waste storage facility yet.'

'You've heard about that?'

'Why are you so surprised?' Malita asks, picking up her wine glass. She raises it to her lips and drinks half. 'You didn't expect that from someone in a lowly service occupation like me, is that it?' She winks. She's got me there.

'Anyway,' she says, 'it's not like I just sit around getting drunk all day.'

She takes another sip. Pushes my glass closer to me.

'So have you heard of the Bülach Reef?' I ask.

Malita shakes her head. I press on: 'They found it quite recently, when they were doing some preliminary drilling for the storage facility. Fossils, corals, all that stuff. It's hundreds of millions of years old, can you imagine? An underground reef!'

Malita's face lights up. She says, 'Back when it first came into existence, this whole place would have been different – you could have lazed around under the lemon trees with the sound of the sea in your ears.'

Again, she slides my glass pointedly towards me. I take a sip. White wine. Much too astringent.

'Yeah, and when we woke up we could have been sipping some delicious drink from a dinosaur egg,' I say.

'Exactly!'

Malita raises her glass to her lips once more.

'I should apply for a job at the facility, once they're advertising,' I continue. 'Kaboom. Waste in, reef gone. Maybe I'll stumble across the fossilised seeds of some ancient primeval lemon down there.'

'Then we'll analyse their DNA,' Malita says. 'We'll breed them and get rich and famous with our Ancient Primeval Lemon à la Szibilla and Malita.' Malita gives a frank and easy laugh.

Then she asks, 'Do you live alone? In the legendary land of Bülach?'

I take a deep breath. 'I'm living in my brother's house. He's upstairs with his family. I'm downstairs.'

'And do you get on alright, you and your brother?'

'We share the same fate,' I say. I hope she can hear it, the irony in my voice. 'It binds us together. It draws us towards the end of something. The village where we grew up is right next to the second possible site for the storage facility. Our dad still lives there. We're going to inherit his house one day. Not bad, as prospects go, eh?'

'Let me guess,' Malita says. 'Your mum lives next door to the third possible site?'

I drink some more of my wine. Two sips. Three. Place the glass back on the table.

'She's not with us any more,' I say.

'Oh, I'm sorry.' Malita's face is close to mine now. I recoil a little.

'Ah, that's just the way it goes. Life. Death,' I say. 'Cancer.'

'So many people struggling with that!' Malita says. 'A cousin of mine was diagnosed with breast cancer last week. It's already metastasised everywhere.' She pauses for a moment. 'It must have been awful for you.'

'Yes,' I say. I'd like to buy Malita another drink, but there's only one nearly empty glass on our table. Mine is still almost full.

'To be honest, I don't really like it,' I say.

'Talking about it?' Malita asks.

'Living with my brother. It's an unhappy house. An unhappy marriage. They're coming to the end of the line as well.' I slide my glass towards Malita. 'And I don't much like this wine, either. Isn't there anything better here? I'm buying.'

Malita wags her forefinger.

'You just have to push through,' she says. 'A little bit more and you'll reach a tipping point. Suddenly the wine will be as sweet as honey. I swear!'

'I'll see what else they have.'

I take two steps towards the bar. Malita grabs my arm. A powerful gesture. Yet caring. 'Why don't we play a round? Yes?'

She stands firm against my gaze. I nod. She swings into motion. Fetches the darts. Positions herself at a distance of two and a half metres from the board. Her first throw hits a bullseye. My turn? Hesitation. A throw – I miss. A second. She throws her head back. Laughs. I hand her the rest of the darts.

'One more!' she says.

I throw. It hits the board – the edge, at least. She presses the wine into my free hand. 'Take another sip! Think of the honey!' Her own glass is empty now. She goes to the bar. Everything about her is in motion. Swift, but never hasty. The bartender refills her glass. As if it's the highlight of his day. Malita returns. Puts down her glass and takes up the darts again. Throws with precision. Another hit. Then she tells me she's only been coming here night after night since she became her mother's mother, to use an over-exaggerated turn of phrase. And I ask, 'Why does she live with you, again?' And Malita: 'It's just not possible.' And me: 'What isn't?' And her: 'Avoiding complications.'

She takes a couple of steps towards the board and yanks out the darts. Comes back. Speaks rapidly, taking little sips from her glass. Her parents emigrated to Switzerland when she was barely out of infancy, she tells me. They wanted to build a better life for themselves. She, Malita, stayed in Portugal for the first years of her life, passed around from one aunt to a grandmother to another aunt. Four years, that lasted. Only then was she taken to Switzerland.

'The early years were terrible. I didn't understand anything, nothing! But eventually I caught on, and then I had to interpret for my parents,' Malita says. She turns to the board. Throws. Hits. And for years she made an interesting mistake. She translated the Portuguese *viver* as 'work'. This did not dawn on her until much later in life.

She looks at me. Throws a dart, blind. It smacks into the wall to the right of the board. Malita does not take her eyes off me. She says, 'That's when I realised: it's true! Life, work, what's the difference?' At least here in Switzerland, she said. At least for her parents, who had grown up doing wage labour, who had no choice in the matter. Who barely had time for anything else. She looks at the board. Throws the remaining dart. A hit. Retrieves the darts. Her father died a few years ago, she tells me. A heart attack. Her mother should have been on disability, but the authorities didn't see it that way. For a long time they insisted she had to be reintegrated back into work. Depression? Back pain? Don't make such a fuss! Well. Now, Malita says, it's too late anyway. Her pension is so tiny that it's barely enough to make ends meet. Hence why Malita has been working here for eighteen months. Not for much longer, though. Her mother is going back to Portugal. Malita raises her glass.

'Cheers. The sad kind!'

She drinks. I want to ask how things are going now. With the depression. How is her mother coping? But better not. There's no bottom to that topic.

'You're slacking!' Malita says, eyeing my glass. There's still some left. 'Guess the honey thing didn't work for you! Oh well. Your turn.'

She hands me the darts. Goes to the bar. I stand alone, in this disgusting room. Walls sticky with sweat and alcohol. Who knows what else.

Malita returns with a full carafe.

'The house wine!' she announces. 'Maybe you'll prefer this one. I'll be emigrating myself, by the way, in three or four years. To Curaçao. I'll teach diving courses and open my own massage practice. Will you come and visit? Anyway, in the meantime we should dance.' She turns her head towards the bar. 'Music! Eddy, you know the drill!'

She knows. She knows what it is, life. The guy behind the bar gives her a wink. He puts something on. So that's it, Malita's sound. A bit gypsy. A bit pop. Buoyant. She moves her upper body to the rhythm. Does a twirl. There is clarity in every fibre of her. The darts are still in my hand.

'Come on, dance!'

I shake my head. Her movements begin to slow and calm. The two guys at the bar have turned towards us now, ogling Malita. I get the urge to throw myself in front of her. She's sweating. She doesn't notice the stares. Or she doesn't care. One of the men gets to his feet. He has a moustache and a leather waistcoat. A heavy silver stud in one earlobe.

'Hey, Maddy. Good mood tonight?' he asks.

Malita does another twirl. Then she turns to face the man. 'Of course, why wouldn't I, with a plus-one like this?' She's taking my hand. Raising it up. Together our hands ball into one fist.

'What's with the vibe in here today? Come on, gentlemen, let your hair down!' she says.

The couple at the pool table give us a bored look. Then they turn back to the game.

Malita has looseness in her blood. She simply keeps on dancing, all across the room. Every now and then, she takes a sip from her glass. Smiles at me. Twirls, hair billowing behind her. The biker follows her with his eyes. I need to get Malita out of here. She is unreachable. Then, abruptly, she is standing next to me.

'Szibilla,' she says, as though completely sober. 'What about you, then?'

'What about me what?' I ask.

'Well, what do you dance to?'

'I can't talk in here. It's too loud,' I say. 'Why don't we go somewhere else?'

'But we've barely arrived!' Malita says. 'Let's dance! We'll talk later! Come on!'

She puts my hands on her sides. Softly. 'Let's relax,' she says. 'You want that, don't you?' I cling to her. Uncomfortable, but not because of her. Why, then? It's the men and their watching eyes. My body, which will not cooperate. I can hardly move. I want her hands all over me, all at once. I pull away. There's a glass on one of the tables. Mine, hers? I drink it down.

'There you go!' Malita cries.

I want to get out of here. I spot the sign for the toilets. When I close the door behind me, I can still hear the music. Then it comes over me, like a tent. The memory. Of the white room. The milky screen. My body strapped down. My body is not asleep. But nor is it awake. I cannot move. I don't want to move. I hear footsteps moving past me. 'Her pulse is too high!' Now I'm shaking, everywhere. I can't stop myself.

I bend down over the basin. I drink. Ice-cold water. I stretch my whole body taut. Wrists under the jet of water. The wooden door. Through it, back into the room. Back to Malita. She's still dancing. Now the second man is on his feet. Staring openly. The biker from before is trying to keep pace with Malita. Trying to dance. There is strength in his arms. I plunge towards Malita. She turns her head to me. Her radiant face. She calls out, 'Szibilla, dance with me!'

I am closer to her, closer.

'Szibilla?'

I can no longer stand. Glimpsing something out of the corner of my eye, I trip and topple forward. Something jabs hard into my side. My head is thudding.

Romi

Eight thirty-one. Leon usually goes to bed early, around eight, or maybe ten past; why hasn't Phil called me back? I read one word, one sentence, close the book, open the next; I flick through the channels on the television – what's the point? There are voices in the corridor, a euphoric yell, shuffling steps. I open the window as a car rushes past; at last, some cool air in the room. I pick up my phone and dial Phil.

'Hi,' he says.

'Hi.'

'You wanted to talk?'

'Yeah,' I say. 'You doing alright?'

'Define "alright".'

'Are you annoyed that I'm calling?'

'I've had a long day. I'm tired. That's all.'

'I want to ask you something.'

'Yes?'

'Do you still love me?'

I hear a noise, the closing of a door.

'Are you still there?'

'Mm,' he says.

'So far it's always been a simple question for us, hasn't it?'

Another moment passes before Phil says, 'Simple? You think so?'

'No, of course not. Not simple, but with a clear answer.'

I wait, and a moment later ask again. 'Can you still say that, then? That you love me?'

Again, silence. Then Phil says, 'No.'

'You don't love me any more?'

'I can't say it right now. Not like this. Not now.'

I swallow. Examine my fingernails, the chewed edges.

'Why not?' I ask.

'It's just – you suddenly wanting to fall back into old patterns like this. You know that's what you're doing?'

'I know.'

I hear Phil's creaking tread on the floor of our apartment.

'It was your choice, and it shook us to the core,' he says. 'Did you think it wouldn't have an impact on how I feel?'

'No, but—'

'Sometimes it seems like you think everything is about you.' He pauses, then he says, 'That's Leon calling again.'

'He's not asleep yet?'

'He's a bit hyper today.'

'Can you call me back? Once he's asleep?'

'I'd rather have a bit of space. I think you spending a couple of days away will be good. For both of us.'

'You don't want to be in touch?'

'Let's take it day by day.'

'And Leon?'

'Romi, it's only five days!'

Another brief pause, then he continues. 'Only three to go. And if Leon wants to call you, then obviously I'll let him.'

'Yeah.'

'I'm hanging up now.'

'Yeah.'

'Goodnight.'

★

I put down my phone. It's hot, leaving a film of sweat on my hand; mechanically I begin to close things: the window, the curtain. I lock the bedroom door. Water gurgles out of the tap; the toothbrush crunches over my teeth. I see Phil, standing poker-straight at that school reunion years ago when we first met, or not quite first; his open face, his expression that betrayed nothing and concealed nothing, the black coat that fell almost to his knees, the shiny buttons that he fastened placidly with his long fingers. And me shifting my weight from one foot to another, waiting for a former school friend – and that's the way it always was, I was always waiting and I always would, for Nora, for Dennis, for Leon, for Phil, and I moved ever more quickly, and the buttons on Phil's coat each like a secret, and I wanted to know all of them, I still want that.

I put my hands to my eyes. My fingers are trembling. My contact lenses end up in the basin, and I don't bother to pick them out. I turn towards the light switch the way I once turned towards Phil – lights out – and to Phil I said, 'I know you!' Origami animals fluttering from the climbing frame and on the school playground. He had been the boy who was always folding paper, and I said, 'Philip!' and he said, 'Phil. When did you start going by Romi?'

My legs carry me to the bed, moving rhythmically and fast, like the second hand; I let myself sink down, give in, give up; my cheeks are hot and the pillow grows damp: these are my traces, the traces of a woman in an airless room. A dark sound comes up from the depths of me, as from an animal, as from a child; that is what I am. I can't get any oxygen, and nothing comes from me except this sound – what woman is left of me now? The child in my belly wants to live, it needs air; I flare my nostrils as wide as I can, but the oxygen does not stream in, it does not reach me. I stand and hunch over – that's better now, that's fine.

I lie back down in bed, positioning myself like Nora yesterday, on my side, legs bent, arms in front of my upper body. My belly rises, falls. Sleep, now.

Szibilla

A strange flat. A strange bed. Malita hands me a sheet.

'There's some more water here,' she says, pointing at the nightstand. On it is a large glass.

'Tomorrow you can stay as long as you like. Take whatever you need. I'll sleep on the sofa so I don't wake you.'

She hesitates. Then she asks, 'Did you book another massage?'

Her silhouette in the dim light. Her voice, as always, clear and steady. No tinge of pity. It's like she's stone cold sober. I nod.

'Sleep well,' she says. 'And I'm sorry if I caught you off guard.'

She switches off the bedside lamp. Goes to the door. 'My mother's name is Beatriz, by the way. I'll let her know you're here.'

She shuts the door behind her and I roll onto my side. I'm tired. And in a strange way, safe. Strange – or simply unfamiliar?

DAY THREE

10 June

Romi

It is a room I'm lying in. It isn't mine. I sit up, push the covers aside; my skull is buzzing. I switch on my phone, which sits heavy in my hand. The display lights up. A text from Dennis. *Good morning! I miss you. Call me?*

I feel sick. I'm so thirsty. My stomach is quiet, entirely empty – where is the baby, why isn't it moving yet?

I need to free myself. The edge of the mattress: a simple white line, a horizontal; I mustn't lose myself, I have to stay. Leon in front of me, in his cot. The blanket is puffy as cotton wool over his little body. He's asleep, thumb in mouth. He knows his mother, a woman who remained what she was, and wholly, not half. A woman who made a decision. Who chose him. Chose her baby. Her children. Her family, before it was too late. My phone blinks. Another text from Dennis.

About the holiday: I promised I'd look into it. I checked yesterday – it'll be easy to travel by train and ferry. The Peloponnese?! Or if you prefer, we could do the mainland instead. Think about it, alright? No rush. You don't have to book anything, maybe just the train to Ancona. I'm really looking forward to it!

I type back, almost automatically: *I can't.*

A few seconds later, Dennis's response: *Is the journey too long? Or is it Leon?*

I can't right now. I need space.

Can we talk on the phone?'

No. It won't work.

Can you text me what's wrong?
I can't.
And in another text: *Everything is against us.*
What?
I'm sorry. I'll be in touch.

I switch off the phone and put it on the bedside table. The room is matte, a single surface, depthless. My contact lenses are still in the basin, shrunken and dry. I rinse them. I see my outline in the mirror, my hips, and put my hands on the widest part. Dough, malleable; I press. Myself: a shapeless thing of bulges, nondescript; small belly, breasts, and what we call a head. A knock. And again. A dull voice.

'Romi?'

I swallow a stringy clod of saliva, smelling as I do my mother's own saliva on a used tissue. She's wiping my mouth as a child; I can't stop myself from retching.

'Just a minute,' I call out. 'Just give me a minute!'

'Did you say something?' Szibilla asks. 'Are you going to let me in?'

I vomit into the toilet bowl. Wipe my mouth. Szibilla is still knocking at the door. I look into the mirror, but I don't really see myself, I see only the flat plane of a woman; but I shut all that down now, I forget it. I tie my hair back tightly, pull on a T-shirt and pyjama bottoms, quickly gargle with water and toothpaste, take a deep breath in and out – 'It is possible to relax,' the midwife said – and open the door to Szibilla. She comes into the room and stops in the middle of it.

'It smells funny in here,' she says.

I sit down on the bed and stretch out my back. Every movement seems to catch, as though my bones, my limbs, no longer fit together properly or slide right at the joints; I can already hear them cracking, and say quickly, 'You took the words right out of my mouth.'

'How are you?' Szibilla asks, and I answer as casually as possible, my voice sounding very far away, 'I've managed to destroy my contact lenses. And I don't have any spares.'

'Glasses?'

I shake my head.

'Do you recognise me?' Szibilla asks.

I stare at her, into what I know to be her face: it's blurred.

'I don't have the first clue who you are,' I say, squinting. My vision sharpens slightly. I see her hair is down, out of character for her.

'Your hair looks like a veil,' I say. 'What are you hiding under there?'

'You see me as a rococo painter? I've broken my hair clip,' Szibilla says with a conciliatory laugh. 'Google it. Anna Dorothea Therbusch. The self-portrait.'

I don't want to, I don't want to move, or to talk, and yet words come almost of their own accord.

'Is there something you wanted to discuss?' I ask. 'Or is it something else?'

'Shall we get some breakfast?'

'Me and you?'

'Are you still upset with me? About what happened the day before yesterday?'

'I mean, you did go straight for the jugular.'

Szibilla tilts her head back slightly, as though thinking. Then she nods almost imperceptibly and asks, 'Did you have a good day yesterday?'

I shrug. Then I say, 'I'm not hungry.'

'Okay,' she says. 'I'll grab you something for later.'

She glances around, then goes over to the window. 'May I?' she asks, then waits for me to agree before she pulls up the blackout blinds and opens the window. Fresh air pours into the room; it's much too bright.

Szibilla turns to me.

'Let's go downstairs. We'll drive into the village,' she says. 'Get some more contact lenses.'

'It's a bank holiday Monday.'

'I'm sure somewhere will be open,' she says. 'It's ten to nine now. We'll set off at half past. It'll do you good to stretch your legs. I'll be waiting outside, alright?'

I shrug again and Szibilla walks out, leaving the door wide open.

Dennis

something is being / sent
No.
something is / sent
No.
something is sent −
something is sent / and I / wait / wait / wait − for Romi

I delete the last four lines, close the laptop and put it down next
to my armchair. A bus trundles by outside. One lone person on
the pavement. A man of fifty-odd in a blue shirt with a white
pattern. He's peering around as though there's something to be
discovered. Now a younger man pushing a buggy comes jogging
along. His long legs carry him effortlessly past the first man, who
stares after him in amazement.

I could tell from the very first moment. The way she stood
there in the café, poker-straight, so ingenuous, with her newspaper under her arm, and so lost. I could tell she was searching, and
she drew me in at once, her green eyes always in a very particular
type of motion − open. they had so much to say, then closed
again, they hid everything. After our first night I also sensed she
would have to send me away, because I had got too close to her.
That it would be difficult. Phil's baby in her belly. Her place in
bed beside him. No, put them aside, those thoughts. The man in
the blue shirt is still standing there, but now he crosses the street,
fanning his face with his hand. His forehead glistens. I stand up

so that I can see further down the road. The man hovers uncertainly by the gate into the park, glancing back and forth. There is still no one on the pavement, no one in the small park, not a single person on any of the benches. No pensioner with a dog, no student with a doorstopper of a book, no young mother with a paper. He walks off, heading to the city centre. Step by step he moves more quickly.

Romi shook her head so firmly, so clearly and explicitly, so free of doubt, as though the question had glanced off her, as if she was catapulting it back as swiftly as possible to me.

She wasn't going to leave Phil, if that's what I was hoping, she said. She wasn't like me.

And when I persisted, she spelt it out: 'I can't do it. Leave everything behind me.'

I should just be happy that she shares with me as much as she does; it will be enough for me, eventually. It will never be enough for me.

No more texts from her. Perhaps that's what this is, then – a separation. Once and for all. There's nothing for me to do but wait here: yellow chair, yellow carpet, bare feet. Wait for what? Not a single cloud in the sky. I open the weather app. It's hot out, apparently, and set to stay that way; the app shows me nothing but little yellow suns, including in the Rhine Valley. I put the phone on the desk. Which – why did I buy it, again? I never work on it. *Something is sent.* I switch the radio on: Love Is in the Air. I switch it off.

Something is sent / and I – but I won't be getting anywhere like that. I stand up, peer into the innards of the flat. My stopgap solution. The two Billy bookcases next to the door that leads into the small kitchen, the bed in the corner. A lone stack of books on the shelf next to the door, a gift from Maxim, ones he's cleared out.

'They're all great,' he said.

I take the top one off the pile: Tomas Espedal, *Go*. I put it next to the others and sift through the rest. Uwe Johnson, *Speculations about Jakob*; Francesco Miciele, *Love in the Time of Climate Change*; Michel Foucault, *Speech Begins after Death*; Paul Auster, *The Invention of Solitude*; Wells Tower, *Everything Ravaged, Everything Burned*; Maggie Nelson, *The Argonauts*. The one female author among all those men, Romi would exclaim, and rightly so. Wasn't she telling me about that book? A black cover, the lettering in white and pink, and below it a quotation from the *Guardian*: 'A book that belongs on the shelves of anyone who desires, especially if what they desire is nothing short of freedom itself.'

I open it, lean against the Billy bookcase, read the first couple of lines.

October, 2007. The Santa Ana winds are shredding the bark off the eucalyptus trees in long white stripes. A friend and I risk the widowmakers by having lunch outside, during which she suggests I tattoo the words HARD TO GET across my knuckles, as a reminder of this pose's possible fruits.

I settle back down in the armchair with a glance out of the window. A group of young people walking along the pavement. They look in high spirits – some clad in heavy hiking boots, others in trainers. I read on.

Instead the words I love you *come tumbling out of my mouth in an incantation the first time you fuck me in the ass, my face smashed against the cement floor of your dank and charming bachelor pad. You had* Molloy *by your bedside and a stack of cocks in a shadowy unused shower stall. Does it get any better?* What's your pleasure? *you asked, then stuck around for an answer.*

I leaf forward and back. Leaf to the beginning again, read it from page one.

Szibilla

She's coming. She's not coming. She's coming. She's not coming.
And if Romi isn't coming, I'll do the massage with Malita instead.
I circle around the rental car. Not a scratch on it. Impeccable.

A bruise on my hip, from where I knocked into the bar yesterday. All because of that one memory? Of the clinic. What the
memory brings with it.

My arm over Malita's shoulders. Her tiny flat. Clean. The
note this morning, next to 'one spotlessly laundered towel', as
she put it, with a winky face. She wrote that I was welcome to
have a shower in her bathroom. A second, strange smiley at the
end of the note. Half head, half heart. I hate sleeping in a strange
bed. Normally.

A brief word with the receptionist was enough. Her name
is Dominique. She made a single call. Good at her job. Bit too
formal, though. And that funny traditional dress.

'Everybody knows everybody here,' as Nora once said.

It's no surprise that Dominique knows Nora. That Dominique's
uncle happens to be an optician. She hung up. 'He'll be home in
two hours. He lives just above the shop in the old town. Just ring
the bell.'

She gave me a slip of paper with the address.

'He's got most of the prescriptions in stock.'

Romi is coming. She isn't coming. She's coming. She isn't coming.
Beatriz on the sofa. Under the ficus tree. The way she nodded at me.

'Sorry. Sorry about that!' she kept saying.

And there I was thinking exactly the same. I was intruding. I was inside her four walls, like a spy. Beatriz got to her feet and returned with a framed photograph: Malita as a schoolchild. Year One? A gap-toothed grin. Already, that liveliness. So captivating it was almost unbearable. So beautiful.

Romi is coming. She's walking through reception. Through the swing doors. I let myself flop into the driver's seat.

Romi

'There you are!' Szibilla greets me; I fasten my seatbelt and catch the scent of something sweet. Suddenly I feel like throwing up again. 'I really don't know why I'm doing this,' I say.

Szibilla starts the car and says, 'What do we ever know about that stuff.'

The engine starts and she depresses the pedal, turning her head to reverse into the car park, one arm around the back of my headrest.

'Is that you, Szibilla Jakab?' I ask.

'You've got that bit right,' she says, turning onto the street. 'What prescription do you need?'

'Minus two point two five.'

'Short-sighted. Oh dear.'

'Could be worse. Do you mind if I get rid of that air freshener?'

'You don't like it?'

'Minus two point two five.'

Szibilla laughs.

'Can we have silence?' I ask. 'Just not talk?'

'I'd rather not.'

'I'd really appreciate it.'

Downhill, my stomach clenching at every bend, as the landscape passes us by. We've long since left Buchenstraße behind us. Nora, years ago in her studio flat, taking a drag of her cigarette and saying, 'Too fat, too thin, too short, too tall, too loud, too quiet, too selfish, too self-sacrificing, too, too, too – I had to hear that my whole childhood, I guess you did as well, right?'

She tapped ash into her empty glass.

'Honestly, I'm grateful to my mum for sending me away, because now I live here and I can do whatever I want. So now I'm pretty much free.'

The houses are growing more numerous: we have reached the village, and Szibilla keeps driving, switching on the radio, some country song, which she turns down the volume on. We drive a little further along the bottom of the valley. All the way around us, every direction we look there are mountains: indistinct but clearly identifiable, and on our right, that must be it, the furthest ridges of the Alpstein, yes, there it is, the Hoher Kasten mountain, nearly 1,800 metres above sea level, and beyond it, invisible from here, the entire mountain range is hiding. The 'mini mountain range'. To the left and to the right there are mountains and nothing but mountains: Alp Sigel, Schäfler, Säntis, Profitis Ilias: unreachable. And then the tears flow, they just do, and I neither encourage nor resist them, and Szibilla hands me a tissue and says, 'Come on. It can't be as bad as all that.'

I blow my nose. Too loud, too grating to cry in here, next to Szibilla, too pathetic, too self-absorbed, too kitsch, and the car rolls to a stop.

'Bannriet,' Szibilla says, climbing out.

Szibilla

There is something of the timid fawn about her. Still, although she hasn't shown it in a long time. She is afraid of me. She moves towards me slowly.

'You don't mind, do you?' I ask. 'If we take a walk here, before we see about the contact lenses?'

She nods. Yes, now she lets herself be led by me. The dams have broken. She must really be upset.

'What's Bannriet?' she asks. She makes a sweeping movement, as though she's been drinking. Behind her is a massive white-and-yellow building. Directly above her head are the words 'THÜR: A suberi Sach'. One enormous car wash.

'There used to be a peat mine here,' I say. I point in the direction of her gaze. 'Until about twenty years ago. These days it's a nature reserve. We need to walk a bit further.'

She lags half a step behind me, head lowered. Parallel to the asphalt road: railway tracks. An Interregio train whooshes past. Between the tracks and the tarmac is a stream. Well, more like a trickle. Then a house, looking like it's in disguise. Something old in new garb. Bright red. Outside, an ostentatious fountain splashing, a girl with a carafe, and next to it a marble table with gilded legs. An automated lawnmower cuts the grass to its precision length.

The houses are fewer and further between. The birches more numerous, their white trunks gleaming. We turn down a gravel track. Now the landscape opens before us, lots of green and brown. The beginning of the Bannriet Nature Reserve.

'Here we are,' I say. 'Still some remnants of nature, mind you. There are storks living here again, and newts, grass snakes. I find it reassuring, to know they'll outlast us all.'

Romi is still walking slightly behind me. She too is glancing around, although I doubt she can see very clearly.

'Humanity is an evolutionary mistake, in my opinion,' I say. 'Our big brains were just a fluke, a point mutation in the genome. Everything on this earth could have been different if that hadn't happened. And it should have been different, I think. It should never have got to the point where us big-brained humans are multiplying and spreading to this extent.'

'Is that why you brought me out here?' Romi asks. More alertly than expected. 'To remind me yet again what you think of my life choices? Of my pregnancy?'

The words are hurled at me – I can almost feel her at my throat.

'Don't worry. I have no ulterior motive.'

We're walking past a field full of ragged yellow-rattle. Tiny yellow calyxes. Sharp jagged leaves, fresh bright green.

I wipe the back of my hand across my brow. Damp. This is how I picture Russia. Part of it, at least. A flat surface. Blazing sun. Pastureland. And beyond, colossal buildings belonging to some nondescript company. Roads. Passing cars. Everything ringed by mountains. A mournful beauty to this obvious failure.

'Have you ever actually loved anything?' Romi asks.

I turn to look at her.

'The linden tree,' I answer promptly.

Romi stares as though I'm speaking a foreign language.

'It was at the edge of the village where I grew up,' I explain. 'According to my father's best guess, it was more than eight hundred years old.'

Romi's expression is intent. She seems to be thinking.

'Did you go there often as a child?' she asks.

'Oh yeah, absolutely.'

'And what did it mean to you, that love?'

'Reliability,' I say. 'For one thing.'

We're still walking. The birch trees seem smaller now. Puny and gaunt.

'What do you mean by that?' she presses.

'The linden tree was constant. That vast trunk. Powerful. Compact. Things come, things go. And the linden grows two centimetres or so each year regardless. That's that. To me, it seemed beyond impressive.'

Romi has nothing to say to that. My forehead is already damp again.

'Can I have a tissue?' I ask.

Romi fishes around in her rucksack and passes me one. I wipe the sweat away.

'Would you say you had a good childhood?' Romi asks. The rucksack is back on her shoulders. I stuff the used tissue into my trouser pocket. 'Definitely,' I say. We walk on. 'Unlike a lot of kids, I had it good. My mother, especially, was a very caring person. She didn't have an easy time of it when she was a child. My father gave her stability, security. I don't know how they pulled it off – a good marriage. They're one of the few examples I know of. One of those rare relationships that worked.'

A stork is circling above us. Legs outstretched.

'I loved my mother,' I continue. 'Genuinely. Which isn't something you can take for granted. Yet even today, it's still an expectation we place on children. They *have* to love their mothers. Both their parents, actually. It's in the terms and conditions. But we don't owe our parents anything! Including love.'

'Are you saying that most people only love their parents out of a sense of duty?' Romi asks.

'Yes!' I say. 'Most parents never really manage to treat their children properly. How many children are beaten, neglected, used to pretend something that isn't true! How many parents don't even see their children! Take Nora as an example. If it was up to her, she'd never have anything to do with her mum. Which I can certainly understand. Anni never had any time for her daughter. Not the slightest genuine interest.'

'So why do you think Nora came here, of all places?' Romi asks.

'I'm sure she'll tell us soon enough.'

Romi plucks at the skin on her forearm with two fingers.

'But back to love,' she says. 'Apart from your mum and the linden tree, is there——'

'I already know what you're trying to get at,' I interrupt. 'You're talking about romantic love. Relationships, that whole can of worms.'

'But you have had some romantic relationships in the past, haven't you?' she asks. 'I mean – what you'd usually term romantic relationships.'

'We can't go any further that way,' I say.

Romi has overtaken me. She's heading towards the woodland that begins at the edge of the track. She pauses.

'We'd better stay on the path,' I add.

She turns to me. Such concentration on her face. It seems as though she truly wants to know.

'Mark.'

'Mark?'

'His name was Mark. But you know that, obviously. As in Mark, the author of the oldest gospel.'

I almost want to laugh but I restrain myself.

'Or alternatively: Mark, meaning "consecrated to the Roman god of war". Five years. Don't tell me Nora failed to mention that.'

'She didn't tell me.'

My Nora. The gravel crunches under my feet. 'There was a constancy to his love as well,' I say. My voice is strong. Thankfully. 'But also something constricting.'

'It wasn't a good relationship?'

'What makes a good relationship in your eyes?'

'Why are you dodging the question?'

'I never wanted a relationship like that. He drew these circles around me. Tighter and tighter, until he got me pregnant. And I lost my mind. So, now you know too.'

Romi nods. Says nothing. Only now do I notice the soft croaking of the frogs in the background. Our personal soundtrack.

'Why should a woman have to explain herself if she doesn't want to live with her boyfriend? She shouldn't have to! He used to ambush me. Grill me for information. "Who were you with? Where did you go?" I barely recognised him in those moments. And the next minute he'd be at the stove, cooking me something. Feeding me. I can't explain to you why I didn't leave sooner. Why I didn't seek help.'

'Did you know Nora back then?' Romi asks.

'I met her after I'd been with him for four years. A few months before the pregnancy. When that happened, I tried to talk myself into it. It'll be great! A child, that's a wonderful thing! But there wasn't any joy. Just panic. The abortion. And then the clinic. The psych ward.'

'This is the first time I've heard any of this, Szibilla.'

We're leaving the woodland behind us. Another path branches off; we forge on straight ahead.

'One thing I did know,' I say. 'Although that really brought it home to me. That we are rootless creatures. Wandering, lost in this world. Searching everywhere for safety. But the way we formulate this desire isn't like that at all. It's completely wrong! And in our error we're destroying not just each other but the Earth as well, in a fundamental way. Even this' – I throw out my arm – 'is a form of deception! Nature? This is basically a museum! Human beings trying to preserve something, some tiny part of what we have destroyed. Three-quarters of the Earth's surface – excluding the parts that are covered in ice – has already been modified somehow. I can even understand it, this impulse to cultivate the land we have shaped. It does us good to ramble around in it. To give a few hares and barn owls a home again. Get back to our roots, so to speak. But all it does is make you *feel* like you're contributing.'

'Haven't you been involved in similar projects, though?' asks Romi.

'A bit, yes, woodland preservation. Childish stuff. A couple of weeks a year. It's fine. But honestly, we mustn't let it hide the fact that it simply doesn't work long term. That human beings consume far too much. More than the planet can provide.'

'And that's why we should wipe ourselves out by ceasing to reproduce?'

'Exactly. There's really nothing so awful about the idea, you know.'

A hide appears in front of us. A simple wooden shed. I step inside. It's dark. A window-like opening at the front overlooks a boggy field, in the middle of which is a pond. Beyond that, more birch trees. A few storks' nests, built on nesting pads supplied by human beings. Romi takes a seat beside me on the bench.

'Some idyll. It's deceptive,' I say. 'Yet it's beautiful too. For the moment.'

A stork lands in one of the nests. It bundles its wings into place.

'I can't tell you how happy I was when I finally saw it in black and white,' I say. 'About a year ago, when I stumbled across an interview with Théophile de Giraud. He was talking about how much more difficult and unlikely it is to be happy than to be unhappy.'

Romi clears her throat. But she says nothing, which I'm glad of.

'People used to give me funny looks. She's burnt out! She's a misery guts. One of *those*! She's too fragile for this world. Can't she just chill out? Romi, you can't imagine how alone I was.'

'What about your friends from before?'

'Apart from my family, Nora was the only one. Although "only" makes it sound … Nora was always loyal to me. Even when everything changed. New job. New flat. Rigid structure. It was the way I had to live. And today I'm living pretty well.'

I put my hand to my right shoulder. A faint stinging pain, running down to my belly and on into my legs. I glance at my watch. I'll be seeing Malita again soon. Then I say, 'But back to relationships for a minute. Would you have started this thing with Dennis if you had loved Phil the way you think love should be?'

'What do you mean?'

'What you said about Dennis. And yourself. It sounds like the typical billing and cooing that leaves no room for anything else. And that's how you've always defined love. Isn't it? As a romantic twosome. Why are you still keeping Phil warm? Out of a sense of duty?'

Romi shakes her head jerkily.

'I'm not keeping anything warm!' she says. 'Hard as it may be for you to imagine, I am attracted to Phil just as much as I am to Dennis. Only, in a different way, yes.'

'So to use your words: what kind of love is it?'

'I see Phil. His beauty, his flaws. Every facet of him. His uniqueness.'

'Like I said: romantic.'

Romi tries to get up, but gravity forces her halfway back down onto the bench. 'Do you really want to know, Szibilla?' she asks. 'Or do you just want to have a go at me?'

Seconds pass. The croaking of the frogs still there – louder, softer. Romi buries her face briefly in her hands. Then immediately pulls herself together. 'I never would have thought I'd be saying this,' she says. 'But you may be right on one score. That it's better to be alone. To be free, for the time being.'

'But even freedom is deceptive,' I say. I gesture to her belly. She rests her hand on it.

'As if freedom were a constant,' Romi says.

'It is. In a certain way.'

'Freedom is a process.'

'For me it's a decision. At least, the freedom we're talking about.'

Romi takes a deep breath. Then she says, 'We are always in some sort of relationship with those around us. It's the only way a certain level of freedom can even exist.'

'You're wrong about that.'

'I understand you find it a difficult thought to entertain. But Szibilla, even you exist in relation to other people, and that's a kind of dependency. There's no getting around it, if you ask me. Luckily, this dependency isn't always as violent as what you experienced with Mark. There can be freedom in it, if there's also trust. Because the other person is a mirror, if I let them be. Because in them I see myself anew, and it allows me to develop as an individual. Collectively, too.'

I shake my head. Say, 'That's exactly why I don't. Establish relationships with others, I mean. Because I don't want that dependency, or the kind of freedom you're talking about.'

'If you don't establish relationships with others,' Romi asks, 'then why are you here?'

I stand up. My legs are pins and needles, on the verge of falling asleep. It's uncomfortable. 'At the beginning of nearly every relationship there's an inherent lack of freedom. It's biology,' I say. 'Or rather, at the beginning of what we call love. Most people wouldn't love their mothers if they hadn't been born unfree. If they hadn't been so dependent on them. And I would never have fallen in love with Mark without the neuro-biological processes in my brain convincing me I had to reproduce. Now I'm fighting back against that sort of dependency. And to do so I use my head. That's where my freedom begins. And nowhere else!'

Romi is looking straight ahead, through the opening in the hide. 'I'm really sorry you got hurt so badly,' she says. 'But I was trying to get at something else. What about friendship? What you and Nora have is also a relationship. Did that also arise out of a lack of freedom?'

'Good relationships are rare,' I say. 'Friendships included. But they are possible. And the relationship I have with Nora is one such rarity.'

I clap my hands against my thighs, one brief hard pat. 'Anyway. Now I'm going to use my independence and take a walk to the old factory building. I need a minute alone. Will you wait here?'

Romi nods.

Phil

The cycle ends, the door opens, the dishes steam, and the cotton cloth is quickly saturated with water. The cutlery basket is heavy; a grain of sweetcorn is stuck between the two tines of a fork. Knives on the right, spoons on the left, forks in the middle. They are covered in a skin of limescale. I've got to refill the salt in the machine. Leon calls out something incomprehensible.

'Just a minute,' I call back. 'Just hang on a minute!'

This excess of cutlery here, and crumbs on the table and streaks on the window and laundry in the living room and paper on the desk. I can picture the one on top, a reading list. I've really got to get cracking, tick things off, put writing on that paper – I'm getting nowhere with anything!

Clean plates out of the dishwasher, stack them in the cupboard. Dirty plates in, flakes of muesli scraped into the compost, water into a glass, I drink. Leon is standing beside me.

'I'm going out to play.'

'Fine.'

'Have you seen my bunny rabbit?'

'He's probably still in your bed.'

'No!'

'Then go look for him.'

'He isn't anywhere!'

Leon is almost shrieking now. Always this searching, always this bending to look under the sofa or behind shelves, always this inexplicable vanishing before our eyes. Nothing in the kitchen, nothing in the hall, chaos in the living room. Playmobil, stuffed animals, books, pillows, all a jumble. As if the flat consisted of nothing but children's things. As if my life consisted of nothing but children. The cardboard boxes – Romi's books and mine – still sitting in the corner. The components of the bookshelf have been removed from the packaging, but that's all.

'Where is my rabbit?' Leon asks.

'I can't see him. Just go without him!'

'No!'

'You know what, he's probably having a little snooze.'

'No!'

'Then look for him!'

'Help me!'

'Look, he's right there!'

'Where?'

'There, next to the sofa.'

Leon picks him up gently and hugs him.

'I'll be right behind you,' I say.

'Outside?'

'Yes, where else? I've just got to get one thing sorted first.'

Romi

I don't see this landscape. I'm not part of it; still, I feel a bit less sick out here. The wood under my hands burnt black by the sun, the head of a nail sticking out. The opening in the hide, 30 centimetres by 120. To the right, miles away, are the mountains of the Alpstein. And somewhere to the left, also in the distance but invisible from here regardless, the Rhine is drawing another border, the border between two countries: one meant to bring order.

I see Nora in my mind's eye, years ago. I see her walk into the classroom and take the first seat she sees, not knowing it was where Vural normally sat, and Vural next to Marc, then Luca, then Martin, then Barbara, Sulamith, Fabienne, then me and so on; Nora didn't know she was upsetting our order, an order we viewed almost as a natural law; and now she had sat down right in the middle of it. Vural came into the classroom and paused, standing behind her. 'Assigned seats?' Nora asked, when Luca instructed her to move. 'Are we in the military or something?' From then on, Luca held a grudge against Nora. He ignored her, and she acted like she didn't notice, including him in conversations, offering to help him with English and maths. In contrast to Luca, Vural had a very special connection with her; he was the only one, apart from me. He was just as delighted as I was by the disorder, the reordering, that she had set in motion. The others admired Nora, a year younger than most of us, with her vaguely unusual dialect; but it was a distant admiration.

'The Rhine Valley? Your accent sounds foreign. Like you're from Austria!' they'd usually say at first, and for the most part Nora ignored it, only once asking, 'Do you guys realise what you're doing here?'

Shoulders shrugged; and at breaktime that same morning, when the two of us were sitting behind the hazel bush, as we often did, Nora said, 'They're the same as the rural kids. Always trying to put everybody in boxes – "from here", "from there". If I live in the city but I speak the Rhine Valley dialect, am I from here or from there? Is Vural from here if he grew up in St Gallen, or is he still from "there", from where his parents were born, before they came to Switzerland to work their arses off? They should drop all that bullshit and look at the *people* instead!'

And as she spoke, she picked the leaves off the hazel bush and flicked them to the ground in front of us.

The clattering of storks' beaks; a spider, millimetre-small, abseiling down onto the windowsill before my eyes. There is no web yet to support it, only this one thread, glittering in the light.

The landscape in front of me: that too seems natural. Yet it is created, shaped by human hands, as Szibilla says: it is system, it is order, like the border between Switzerland and Austria, like the assigned seats in the classroom, like the nuclear family, like the opportunities open to individuals in a society.

At nursery and primary school, there were still lots of kids from what we called 'migrant' families, the obvious kind: Derya, Aziz, Fatma, Dilip and Zaina (Christian with his Dutch mother and Thomas from Bavaria were not visibly 'foreign' enough to count). When they split us up by ability, only Derya and Vural stayed in my class. The others were put on a different track. Vural was the only one who continued on to upper secondary.

'And why? Because equal rights is a foreign concept!' Nora said, and later Phil said it too, in a different way. Little by little, Nora and I began to understand that these things were anything but random; as the years went on, we gained a better understanding of what it was, a structural problem, a manufactured order; but Nora was one step ahead of me right from the start. Our seating arrangement in class was punctured the minute she entered the room. Still, I sat next to her whenever I could, next to Nora, and I wasn't Romina any more, I was Romi.

And who am I now, in this little cubbyhole? I gaze into the out-of-focus countryside, then snap a picture on my phone. I can see the bristly field on the screen now, clear in outline. Luminous green, a few dots of violet.

Another picture – that must be it, the old peat factory. It looks as though several rickety wooden sheds were squashed together and merged into a single building. It feels oddly calm, as though it were the most inevitable thing about this place, and yet alien: something fallen out of time. The roof of the main building rises to a peak like the mountains behind it; surely it has been here for a long time. It is shrouded in something dark, something like a shadow – but the shadow of what? In front of it, between the factory and the hide, at the bottom edge of the photograph, unmistakeable, striding her way back to me: Szibilla in her zebra-patterned sunglasses and black shorts, which glint in the sun.

Szibilla

We're a fart, we humans. Our whole history: a tiny *phut*. I do my best to imagine it. That thousands of years ago, this whole place was 180 metres deep beneath a glacier, carving out the valley. Infinitely slowly. Eventually it melted into a vast lake. Then, it dwindled, until at last it split in two. The Rhine Valley Lake and the primordial Lake Constance. Plant material, partially decomposed, settled underneath the water and compacted into peat. One millimetre per year. The Rhine Valley Lake disappeared. Only the Rhine remained, and Lake Constance. Alluvial forest grew. Fenland formed. The pre-alpine hills were overrun with trees. A paradise for animals and plants. Then human beings came increasingly to dominate, and all of a sudden time sped up. We carved vast-scale topographies from the natural world. And within a few decades, we dug out the nine-metre layer of peat that had taken nine thousand years to form. To dry it. To burn it. To heat our parlours. All for that!

Something moves. Romi's head in the hide. Probably working away like a madwoman in there.

I walk around the bend. Reach the hide. Step in. Sit down next to Romi.

'You should go and have a look as well. The old peat factory,' I say. 'Great place to refresh one's understanding of humanity. Remind ourselves where we come from. Where we're going. Where we should go.'

'Those are big questions for a bank holiday Monday,' Romi says.

'Look who's talking.'

Our eyes meet. Romi squints, as if she's trying to focus on me. For a moment it looks as though she's about to burst out laughing. I'm on the verge of it too – but we don't.

'It's not pessimistic, you know,' I carry on, 'seeing yourself as a component of the world, in context with other components. It's realistic. Lightens things up a bit.'

'Is that how you feel?' Romi asks. 'Light?'

'What's changed is that these days I face facts. Instead of letting them steamroll me.'

Romi is fiddling with something on the ledge under the window. 'There's one thing I really don't get,' she says at last. 'If you've genuinely been able to leave all that ballast behind you, and now you've reached this point of clarity, like you're saying – why aren't you a bit more laid-back about things? To me you seem anything but lightened up.'

I hesitate. Then I say, 'That's just how it is, being human. I've tried explaining it already. How rare happiness is.'

'Look, I'm going to ask you straight out,' Romi says, 'and please don't take this the wrong way. I'm only asking because I'm genuinely interested. Why don't you kill yourself?'

She turns to face me. 'I'll answer that in the spirit of Théophile,' I say. 'Because it is a task. To guide the people who are already here onto the right track.'

'Bit left-field, that perspective,' Romi says.

'If you think it through to its logical conclusion, it's not that left-field. Anyway, you'd be surprised how many people hold a similar opinion. The Birth Strikers in England. The childfree movement. The political anti-natalists. Fridays for the Future is moving in the same direction, actually. These days lots of people have decided to opt out of expanding the human population. Which also means opting out of the suffering that life inevitably entails.'

Romi appears to let the words sink in. Then she says, 'You said yourself that once a baby is born, we should give it the best possible life. But you haven't said anything about what that actually means to you. What is "the best possible life"?'

'I mean a stable environment,' I say. 'Someone to care for them. Parents who take an honest look at their child, who see them as they really are. Parents who don't try and force anything. But that's pie in the sky, really, so it's better not to bother.'

Romi doesn't reply. She's staring awkwardly into space.

'Are you worried about your children?' I ask.

Slowly she shakes her head and says, 'No, I wasn't thinking about that. It's just – when I'm around you, everything seems so pointless somehow.'

My trainers scrape back and forth across the gravel. I don't want this, but it's happening. My restless leg is back. Impossible to stop.

'It feels like this notion of humanity eradicating itself has become your sole purpose in life. But there must be something else, Szibilla, surely? In your life? Something specific, I mean?'

'Please don't,' I say. 'Please let's take a step back.'

Romi turns to look at me. She is surprised, obviously so. Her mouth has shaped itself into a tiny 'o'. 'Silence after all, then?' she asks eventually. She gets to her feet. Peers around, intently.

A family of ducks has alighted on the pond, the female near the bank. She tugs at something, surrounded by her ducklings. Eventually, she lets go. She has caught nothing.

Romi

Dusty cobwebs underneath the beams on one side of the building. Looks like some further up, as well, below the roof tiles – I can just make them out. The knotholes in the wood are bright, as though the sun is using all its might to penetrate the little hide. Yet inside all is cool and dark. Cool as Nora's body in repose.

Szibilla gets to her feet. 'Right,' she says. 'We'll go back.'

She walks out of the hut. I follow; the sun is high in the sky.

'Did Nora ever say anything to you about regretting Meret?' I ask.

Szibilla waits another pace or two before she answers. 'She went back and forth about it from day one. That's why she didn't tell me about it until quite late on. The pregnancy, I mean. It's different with you. She knew I'd react more sceptically.'

She isn't going back the way we came. She's taking a different route, perhaps a loop.

'Every once in a while, something would come blurting out,' Szibilla says. 'It started before she'd even given birth. Saying she couldn't do it, she couldn't handle it.'

'She never breathed anything to me about having doubts. Not a word!'

I shield my eyes with my hands and walk a little closer to Szibilla, trying to get a better look at her face.

'I just really want to help her,' I say.

'She doesn't need it. She's helping herself. After it's done, she'll feel better. She'll see things more clearly. Everybody gets there at some point. Sooner or later.'

Szibilla pauses briefly to look around, at this countryside, at this something, and suddenly I feel as though I'm close to her, as though I recognise something in her searching gaze.

'Even when I was a child, sitting underneath that old linden tree,' she says, 'I felt it. That I was missing a need to exist. For all human beings to exist. To take the paths they take on this planet. Daughter behind mother behind mother behind mother and so on. But I needed my little detour so that I could see things clearly again. And I can't deny, it was utterly exhausting. There are things I wish I could have spared myself.'

'Did you spend a long time at the clinic?' I say.

'A couple of weeks. Why do you ask?' She glances at her watch. 'We could go and pick up your contact lenses.'

We walk around the old factory building. I snap a photograph and examine it. From the side, the crooked, shed-like buildings that make up the tangled whole are even easier to see than before. The wood is dark brown, nearly black; the tiled roofs are steeply sloped and weathered. A birch tree grows in front of the tallest building, its uppermost branches ending just below the gable: a pale hand reaching for the dark.

I flick the image away and raise my head. It's unreal, this landscape, a single plane; only photographs give me a glimpse of what is concrete here, what there is to find. Order-disrupting, order-creating. I'd like to go inside, really, I'd like to examine it more closely: the insides of it, its shadows.

Szibilla walks on, and I stay beside her. We reach the rental car in silence and open the doors, struck by a wave of heat. Instantly the nausea is back. Szibilla starts the engine.

Phil

Three bags of flour, all opened. Where's the yeast? Nothing in the fridge. Open the cupboard: a bag of dry yeast.

'Can I help?'

I give Leon a nod and he points to the bag in my hand. I tear it open, and he shakes the yeast into the bowl. We fill a measuring jug with water, and Leon misses, pouring half of it onto the counter. Again we fill it up, and the dough wells up between my fingers, and Leon's fingers, in the bowl.

'Is it for lunch?' he asks.

'It's for dinner,' I say. 'Pizza.'

'I'm hungry!'

'Give me a minute and I'll make you a sandwich.'

'When is Mama coming home?'

'She's not coming home today. She's on holiday with her friends until the day after tomorrow. You know that.'

'But pizza is birthday food! Isn't Mama celebrating with us?'

'What? Nobody's having a birthday.'

'But pizza is only for birthdays!'

'Well, today we're having a visitor.'

'Is it Nanna?'

'It's a colleague.'

'What's a colleague?'

'Her name is Chiara. We work together at the university.'

'So is she your friend?'

'You could say that.'

'Is she a friend, yes or no?'

'Yeah, sure.'

'Is she nice?'

'Absolutely. And Leon, if I let you watch some *Paw Patrol* after your sandwich, can you give me a bit of time to read something in my office, please? It's very important now.'

He considers this. He nods.

'Chiara and I need to get some work done while she's here. You can go to Nanna's in the meantime. Then you'll come back for pizza. Alright?'

'Will Chiara still be here then?'

'I think so, yes.'

'Okay.'

Romi

My bare feet on the rough carpet. It's the same as this morning, as yesterday; even the smell in my room is slowly becoming familiar. Two fourteen. The box of contact lenses is as big as my palm, it's as big as the partial map of Berlin on my notebook; I'll put them in later. I don't want to see in focus yet.

'We'll have another room ready for you in two hours,' said the receptionist just now, Dominique. I have her to thank for the contact lenses, according to Szibilla, and I shook my head and said, 'There's no need.'

I felt Dominique's eyes on me more than I saw them. She seemed to be checking whether I was the same person she'd seen that morning, Romina Bertschy, known as Romi; she seemed to be wondering why I wasn't happier about moving to a larger room, about getting hold of new contact lenses on a bank holiday, about the Rhine Valley sun, beating down fiercely from the sky.

The book containing Susan Sontag's long-form interview is on the floor. I lie down next to it. Sontag was a mother too, a lover, a seeker, always was; a woman who spoke.

NOTE

Number of definitions of love: …
My definition of love: …
Number of people who are important to me, whom I love: …
Moments that spontaneously come to mind when I think of love:

Hiking with Phil at the very beginning of our relationship, when I closed my eyes and let him guide me hundreds of metres, and heard nothing but the singing of the birds.

Dancing with Nora, years ago, when the dance floor suddenly emptied and only the two of us were left, facing one another, not even any music, or so it seemed to me; and all at once the dancing seemed to happen of its own accord, an extraordinary power in my hips, and such closeness, to Nora and to myself.

With Dennis, our second meeting, when I was all dishevelled, and he said, 'You're looking to explore the vastness out there, aren't you?' And I felt so seen, from top to toe, and I said nothing in reply because nothing was needed.

With Robert, in the garden, spring. I was eleven years old. Carrot seeds in my father's palm, and I drew a line in the soil. 'Not too deep!' he said. 'The seeds need light to sprout!'

Leon in my lap. 'Sing!' he says, again and again. 'When are you going to sing to me, Mama? When are you going to sing?' His little hands clapping together, smeared in sauce and slobber, and I can't help but laugh, and he says, 'Sing! Sing! Again!'

Number of moments contrary to these, which come to mind when I think of the silence long ago, in my childhood flat, at school; of the not-speaking, of the great silence of families, of my family's silence: …

THE GREAT SILENCE

My mother sits at the kitchen table, hunched. A trembling runs through her body, a trembling that breaks off when I sit beside her, at my empty breakfast bowl. Before I can say anything, I see my mother's eyes, red-rimmed; 'Eat now,' she says. Opposite her is my father's coffee cup, filled to the brim, his chair pushed back, tilted. 'Eat!' my mother says. The flakes of oat taste dry, the trembling returns:

my mother is shaking, and I want to ask her where my father is, but instead I chew the flakes to slime and swallow.

THE GREAT SILENCE II

Following my father through the school as though I were his shadow. The corridors are dark, his footsteps echo. He's walking his familiar route, beginning with the toilets, scrubbing the floors, oiling the door. Then he moves in the direction of the gym. Pauses on the way, level with the library. Opposite the door leading to the books is the door leading to classroom 3A. It's stuck all over with drawings. At the very top is the heading 'My Family'. In the drawings, scrawled in coloured pencil: Mama, Dada, child. Most of them depict a family outside a house, smiling faces, waving hands.

I'm twelve years old. I'm in 6B. If I were still a younger child, my drawing would be of the same thing: Mama, Dada, child in front of a house, smiling faces, waving hands. But behind it is another picture: a man, a woman and a child sitting at a round table, all three heads bowed, the ends of their hair dangling into the soup tureen before them.

THE GREAT SILENCE III

In the fridge, top shelf, are the slimline products my mother has been eating lately. Slimline yoghurt, slimline margarine, slimline cheese, slimline milk, slimline ham. In the bathroom cabinet, bottom shelf: a powder compact, a black eye pencil, still unused, and next to it a sharpener.

THE GREAT SILENCE IV

My father turns to me. Puts a finger to his lips. We enter the caretaker's room, the room that's just for him: vacuum cleaner, mountains of rags, tools. He presses a bottle of Orangina into my hands and clinks it with his. The drink tastes sweet and tingles on my tongue. My father says, 'This is my favourite place.' He gestures deeper into the room. Only now do I realise there is a narrow passageway leading to a second, smaller room.

In this room there is a small knee-high table, and on that an intricate tablecloth and several decorative metal trees: a hornbeam, a sycamore, a fir, a pine, an ash. Plain candles are arranged around them, packets of incense sticks, a holder. Before the altar there is a thin raffia mat. Crushed beer cans. 'Lovely, isn't it?' my father says. He puts an arm around my shoulders. 'I wanted to show you. But we can go back to bed now. Your mother doesn't need to know anything about it.'

THE GREAT SILENCE V

I place my hand on Robert's back. I feel a pulse that's growing stronger, warmer too, then I turn away.
'I've decided to leave here now. I wish you all the best!' I say, and I walk back down the dark corridor and through the door that leads outside, and there's my mother with a cigarette in her hand and high-heeled shoes. She smiles and waves me over. She is young. She is tall. Her denim skirt cuts into her belly. Her chest rises and falls.
'Exactly!'
I walk up to her and ask, 'Did you say something?'
'Exactly!' she repeats. 'And now you're coming to me!'

I put the pencil down. Then I reach for the phone and dial my mother's number. It rings twice before she picks up.

'Hi Romi, how's it going?' she asks, obviously delighted.

I can't get a word out.

'Romi?' she says again.

'Where are you?' I ask.

'On the train. On my way back from a training course.' It sounds like she's chewing something now, a bit of apple, gum, her fingernails, and I ask, 'How are things?'

'Good! Today was great. And I hear you're in the Rhine Valley? How's everything with you, then?'

'What did Robert tell you?'

'Just that you were asking him questions about the old days.'

'Do you remember much about that time?'

For a moment my mother says nothing. Then she asks, her voice unchanged but a little less buoyantly, 'About his affair, you mean?'

I hesitate. Then I say, 'Yes.'

'Of course I remember '

'I'd be really interested to hear what you think about all of that today,' I say.

Pause. 'It was a long time ago,' my mother begins, 'and obviously these days I'm seeing it from a very different standpoint.' She seems to be thinking. 'I was very hurt by it all. Not so much that Robert fell in love with someone else, but all those months he lied to me. When I found out, he kept promising he'd end things with the other woman. But it didn't happen.'

She breaks off.

'And eventually you gave him an ultimatum,' I say.

'Yes. If you don't take action now, I'll make the decision for you. And if you leave it up to me, you'll have to go.'

'Would you still do the same thing today?'

Silence at the other end of the line. Again, that chewing.

'Are you eating?' I ask.

'Mixed nuts,' my mother says, with a laugh. Her voice is more serious again as she continues: 'I have no interest in regret. It is what it is, now. We're doing well, your father and I.'

'What does that mean?'

'We have a good life. We've found our groove together,' she says, emphasising the word *together*. 'It wasn't always that way, as you know. But remember, when your father started his affair,

I had no real education. He was the one with an income, and it was his job that got us the flat in the school building, which was really very cheap.'

She pauses again briefly, then says, 'To be honest, I didn't have very many options at the time.'

I picture my mother on the train in her denim skirt, bag beside her, bare feet on the seat opposite, one hand squashing the phone to her ear and the other buried in a bag of sultanas and nuts; as though she were a young woman, one I was only just getting to know.

'I wanted to go to therapy, but he only came with me once,' she said. 'He lived in parallel worlds while he was carrying on with Tana. And as I said, that was the thing I found hardest of all.'

'But it wasn't any better afterwards.'

'The first years were awful, that's true. We had to build up a sense of trust again, step by step. It took a long time. You know, Romi, I think it's brave, what you and Phil are trying to do. I don't know if I could have done it back then. But I wouldn't have dismissed it straight off the bat. As long as it didn't involve lying.'

'Are you telling me this today because you're in a good mood?'

'Why do you ask?'

'You haven't said a single word about Phil, Dennis and me until now.'

'You never asked! It's none of my business, after all, it's yours. Yours and theirs.'

I swallow nothing.

'It was a difficult time for me, you know,' I say. 'Your silence. And you were so incredibly far away.'

For a moment she says nothing. I'd love to be able to see her expression. Is she pensive, nervous, bored?

'Yes. I imagine it was,' she says.

And after another short silence, as though to cheer me up: 'But there were other moments too. Going shopping together on Saturdays. You always nabbed the biggest croissant!' I wait. Nothing else is forthcoming.

'When I think about those days, you're not there,' I say at last. 'Not really.'

'I'm so sorry.'

She waits. Then she asks, 'How are you getting on with your friends?'

'It's all a bit complicated. I'll give you another call soon, okay?'

'Oh right, yes. Look after yourself. I love you.'

I roll onto my back; the second hand in the clock above the bedroom door is ticking more slowly, and the noises from the corridor outside have fallen quiet. Already past four. Can I really have been in here for two hours, again?

Take detours, Szibilla said. To get some clarity on things. I hear her voice, the stress she placed on the nouns: *Daughter behind mother behind mother behind mother*. I repeat: Child behind parent behind parent behind parent. I cannot change it.

Soon I will feel the baby in my belly for the first time, like I did with Leon on the night train from Hamburg after that holiday with Phil on the North Sea coast, our last as just the two of us. It was beautiful, familiar, but the whole time I'd felt physically unwell, bloated, as though my skin had gone slack, and as I lay there on the narrow bed, expecting nothing but a jolting, troublesome night, I felt a sudden movement in my belly – a new life, a tiny creature growing day by day, growing beyond itself, beyond me, like the new baby is now. It won't be long before the baby is outside of me, gazing at me with its big eyes, and at first it will believe everything I say, just as I believed Robert and my mother when I was a child; and this heritage is part of me still – a part of my skin.

I close my eyelids. My stomach growls. I should eat something, now. Four thirty-seven, up and out of the room.

Szibilla

Black leather of the chair beneath me. White wall before my eyes. The grey shelves attached to it. The textbook is exactly where I left it yesterday. Ovaries, fallopian tubes, uterus, vagina. Below the books, in the basket: colourful board games. A huge collection. A box of dice. Monopoly. Everything in a jumble. Littered on the floor beside it are playing pieces in an array of colours. Wooden snails. Nobody is keeping the place tidy.

'Have you recovered from last night?' Malita asked me just now.

'I didn't drink that much,' I said.

'That's not what I meant.'

Malita's hands, patting. Stroking. Kneading. Feeling their way. Ravensburger 4 First Games. Scrabble. Romi would be into that. She wouldn't make individual words, she'd make phrases. THE BEST LIFE. With a question mark at the end. Then she'd look at me, expectant. My earlier answer wasn't enough. Not for her. Or for me.

I take my phone out of my pocket. I can't find anything with a quick search. No articles that I haven't seen already. Then to YouTube. A new film, two minutes. Théophile de Giraud seated in a dark room, filming himself. 'Why am I an anti-natalist?' he asks. Today he doesn't want to get tied up in philosophy – he'd rather focus on the ugly facts of reality. Lately, he says, he's started snoring. A couple of hours ago he woke up his wife, so he banished himself to this little room. And in here he won't get any more sleep, despite the help of alcohol.

The camera pans. An arsenal of bottles appears. The camera pans back. Théophile hasn't moved. Big eyes. Earnest gaze.

'That tells you something,' he says. 'We bother other people even in our sleep. And even in our sleep, they bother us. Even people we love. Life is hell. Even with the best of intentions, it will always be hell.' And that's why he's an anti-natalist. He nods into the camera. Conclusively. Knowingly.

I let out a guffaw. He's serious. And he has a sense of humour about it too. Both at the same time. I wipe my hand over my lips. The phone rings. Romi.

'Hey, I'm heading down to the dining room,' she says. 'Are you coming?'

'Sure,' I say. 'I'll be right there.'

Romi

The fork slips through the tart, and everything finds its way into my mouth, onto my tongue, one layer after another: cream, crust, raspberry, vanilla cream, sour cherry; the flaky pastry crunches between my teeth. Opposite me, Szibilla is flicking through a book on the Bödmeren Forest: 'The last old-growth forest in Switzerland,' she told me earlier, before returning to her book.

Every now and then, she looks up to spoon chocolate pudding into her mouth, holds it on her tongue for a moment, concentrating, then swallows and is lost again in the book. I eat as though it's my first time. My hunger is immense and so is my appetite. I fill my glass with water – Szibilla's too – and drink, focusing on the back of her book. On it is a thick-trunked tree viewed from below, looking up towards the crown. Beyond the canopy of leaves is a sky of shimmering blue.

'Have you ever been to the Bödmeren Forest?' I ask.

'Yes.'

'Would you recommend it?'

'Absolutely.'

She turns another page, smooths it flat and adds, 'It's karst terrain, a very expansive kind of landscape. Seamed with fissures and sinkholes. Downy birches growing out of the hollows in the rock. I'd like to go back.'

She stretches and immediately clutches her right shoulder.

'Are you having a massage today?' I ask.

'I've already had it.'

'Was it good?'

'My back feels better than it has in years.'

'And your period pain?'

'Almost gone.'

'Hallelujah.'

'No, it's thanks to Malita.'

'Is that her name, the massage therapist?'

Szibilla nods and goes back to her book. I take the last bite of raspberry tart and lean back in my chair. Only three other tables are occupied, all of them by the window. The waitress is gliding more than walking through the space, serving coffee at one table, taking orders at another, then vanishing behind the bar.

Suddenly, again, I'm feeling sick. I put a hand to my stomach and sit still; Szibilla is reading, her eyes following the tracks left by the letters, leaping from line to line. I hold my breath. Exhale slowly. Then I take out my phone and examine the pictures I took this afternoon. The flat expanse. Szibilla in front of the old peat factory. The old peat factory itself.

I bring up Google and type in *Bannriet old peat factory*.

Szibilla

Romi keeps glancing up from her phone. Sometimes at me. Sometimes out of the window.

'It's funny,' she says at last, 'that you can't see Bannriet from here.'

We go out onto the terrace. I show her. There's the nature reserve. There's the old factory. But yes, she's right, it's hard to see from this distance.

We gaze out for a while. Unclouded skies. Such shimmering, everywhere. Small animals, cars.

'How about a film?' I ask eventually.

Romi seems dubious.

'Or did you have something else in mind?' I prompt.

'No,' says Romi. 'I think a film night sounds like a pretty good idea.'

'*A Pigeon Sat on a Branch Reflecting on Existence.*'

'That's the title?'

'Yup.'

'How poetic.'

'My room. Thirty minutes, let's say?'

Romi nods. We go back into the dining room. It's filled up. Dinner time. Our cake plates have already been cleared. A waitress comes over to our table.

'Can I bring you anything else?'

I order two sandwiches to go. Give them my room number.

'It's on me,' I say to Romi.

'Thanks. See you in a bit.'

I take the lift. This isn't ordinary fatigue. My feet are heavy. Getting to my room, I open my laptop. Take off my shorts. They smell of sweat. Of the day. Of my period. Bathroom – light on. The fan hums. I sit down on the toilet. Tampon out, tampon in. How I hate it, my fingers in those slack places.

'I wanted to apologise,' I said to Malita this afternoon. I was on the couch. Surrendered to her. 'About the blood yesterday.'

'It's nothing,' she said simply.

I flush. Wash my hands. Go back into the room. My laptop asks me for my password. DeGiraudNow! The dissected fibroids on the screen. I close the window, put the file in a folder marked Bits & Bobs. I plug in the external drive. It swallows the DVD without demur.

Phil

Leon pulls the waistband of his pyjama trousers up to his belly button. Then he gets into bed. I put the rabbit next to him and he reaches for it at once.

'Dada, is Mama really at a hotel or is she sleeping at Dennis's today?' he asks.

'At a hotel,' I say. 'She's still on holiday with her friends.'

'Is Chiara sleeping here today?'

'No.'

'Where does she live?'

'In Zurich.'

'But that's so far!'

'It's just a train ride.'

'Is Dennis coming here today?'

'No.'

'Where is he?'

'In St Gallen, I suppose. At home.'

'Is he a friend or a colleague?'

'What is he to you?'

'A friend.'

'Would it upset you if Chiara stayed the night?'

Leon shakes his head. 'She's a friend too, you said so.'

His voice, old beyond his years. I switch off the light.

'That's true,' I say.

'Don't you want to stay at Dennis's sometimes, like Mama does?'

'No, I don't think so.'

'Why not? Isn't he your friend too?'

'Good question.'

'So is he your friend or not?'

'Alright, my lad, I think that's enough big questions for one night – sleep well.'

He rolls from one side to the other.

'I love you,' he says.

'Love you too. Good night!'

'Good night.'

I step out into the hall, past the unused standing lamp, the over-stuffed bags of baby clothes. The plan, supposedly, is to put them either in the attic or in the wardrobe. But neither Romi nor I have touched any of them. Tomorrow I'll unpack a few boxes, definitely.

I slide open the balcony door. Chiara is outside, leaning slightly back in her chair, her feet resting lightly on the railing. She has lit a cigarette, and asks if Leon is asleep. I nod. 'Almost. Light one for me as well?'

'You smoke?'

'Just for today, with you.'

'You need it?'

'Mm.'

She smiles, taps a cigarette out of the pack, puts it between her lips, lights it and passes it to me.

'Enjoy.'

I take a drag. Immediately the nicotine makes me dizzy. A knot of people has formed in the garden – Vinzenz is having a barbecue. A bonfire lit, soft music playing.

'I honestly can't believe how long the glass-free solar panels took,' I say. 'We could be miles further down the road by now!'

'Come on, let's leave work at work,' she says. 'You've got a nice place here, you really do. And so peaceful, too.'

I ask if I've already told her that I was born in this village. And that I lived here until I started school. Chiara shakes her head. Her fawn-brown hair moves with it. I say I never imagined I would one day live here.

'You inherited the flat, right?'

'Yes,' I say. 'After we moved away, I used to come here often to see my grandmother. Sometimes, when I watch Leon hugging his stuffed animals or chewing his vegetables for ages or perfectly positioning his Playmobil figures, I see myself. To be honest, I'm not sure it was such a good idea to move here.'

Chiara turns to me. She has pushed all her hair to one side. Only now do I notice the tomato stain on her top, just where I think a nipple must be.

'So where is your wife right now?'

'Romi's on holiday with some friends.'

'It's cool that you're giving her the chance to do that.'

'I mean, of course I am.'

'A lot of men wouldn't. Most of my female friends have to do absolutely everything. The household work, mainly looking after the kids, taking on the whole mental load and so on, plus some of them have jobs as well, let's say 20 per cent – but not so much for themselves, more so that the kids get to have a day with Daddy. At least, that's how it seems to me sometimes.'

'Switzerland is lagging behind when it comes to family,' I say, adding that in a recent UNICEF study, it came in last place. 'I'm not surprised!'

'Last place worldwide?' Chiara asks.

'Out of thirty-one European countries. If I worked at a university in Germany, I'd earn less money, but I'd get parental leave. Not just one day. *Holiday!*'

'I heard there's a movement starting to push that issue. A petition for more parental leave,' Chiara says, and takes a puff of her cigarette. Slowly she blows the smoke high into the air. 'I've got to hand it to you, you're a very progressive man.' She laughs. 'Sorry. That sounds dumb. But I mean it.'

I hesitate. Then I say it. 'I don't have a choice.'

Chiara gives me a probing look. 'What do you mean?' she asks.

I should have been expecting that question. 'I'm not sure how to put it,' I begin. I put the cigarette to my lips and inhale, but the time I buy myself doesn't help. 'It's actually pretty simple, really. Romi and I are in a – well, a transitional phase, let's say. She's got another man.'

'Oh really? Is it just a sex thing, or what?'

'For her it's more than that.'

'A second relationship, then,' Chiara says, glancing at me sidelong. I turn to look at her.

'So that means we could have some fun tonight as well, right?' she continues. 'Jump into bed?'

She giggles, but it's not a childish sound, it's bolder than that. What should I say?

'You're not just a progressive dad, you're a sexy dad as well,' she says, then quickly puts her hand over her mouth. 'Oh no,

I'm just digging myself in deeper. Now I'll have to talk myself out of it somehow.'

She pauses, not looking remotely embarrassed. The way she takes a drag of her cigarette, observant eyes still fixed on me. Then she asks, 'You're still running the show here, though, right?'

I put my feet up on the railing too. One of Vinzenz's guests has changed the music to electro swing. What time is it, I wonder.

'No answer is still an answer,' Chiara says.

'I thought those were all rhetorical questions.'

'Not at all!' she says, flicking her cigarette ash over the balcony.

'They're having a good time down there,' she says, gesturing to the party in the garden. The first few people have started dancing. Women, mostly. The rest of them – all men – are standing around the fire with their feet planted wide, each with a beer bottle in his hand.

'Slowly but surely, I'm getting fed up of city life,' Chiara says. 'And not just because of the rent. At the end of the day, no matter where you go, you're just bumbling around inside the same perpetual bubble. All that city bullshit is getting tedious. I'd rather be doing a bit of gardening!'

She stubs her cigarette out on the stone floor. Takes another one out of the pack, puts it between her lips and lights it.

'We could do a swap,' I say. 'Sometimes I feel like I wouldn't mind going back to the city.'

One of the party-goers launches into a noisy attempt at a song, his voice sliding into an uncontrolled bawl. The group roars with laughter.

'But you've got such wonderful neighbours here!' Chiara says.

We both laugh.

'I lived in Zurich while I was a student,' I say. 'And I think I'd have stayed there, if it wasn't for Romi.'

'Do I hear a hint of regret?'

'No.'

'Not even the tiniest trace?'

'Wrong question.'

'Okay. Do you have anything else to drink?'

'Out here in the sticks, all we drink around this time of night is tea.'

Chiara jabs her thumb in the direction of the carousing neighbours and says, 'Sounds like you want me to hang out with them instead.'

'Would you?'

'Sure!'

She's noticed it now too, the stain on her blouse. She rubs at it, the burning cigarette clamped in her mouth. Her breast jiggles up and down.

'Alright then. I'm going downstairs to grab a beer with that lot, then I'll head home,' she says, rising.

'No, wait. I've got something better. Walnut schnapps. If you're into that sort of thing?'

She nods.

Romi

Szibilla pushes the laptop into the trough between her thigh and mine, then shuffles into a comfortable position on the bed. The title of the film fades in, then the words: 'The final instalment in a trilogy on the human condition'. White lettering on a black background. The music quietens. Scene one. A man is standing by a table laid ready for a meal, while a woman is busy in the kitchen. There is music, and the woman hums along. The man is trying to open a bottle of wine, but as he struggles, he has a heart attack and drops dead. The woman is still humming. Next scene.

Szibilla is gazing mesmerised at the screen; beyond her is the windowpane, the wooden balcony, and from there my gaze drifts onward into the valley. I let myself sink deeper into the pillow. A group of flamenco dancers, one man among women. The teacher keeps going up to him, touching him, but he pushes her hands away. Cut to a woman sitting on the floor in the corridor outside, cleaning. The flamenco dancers' shoes are still audible next door. The sitting woman makes a telephone call. 'It's nice to hear you're doing alright,' she says, again and again. A door opens, the male flamenco dancer rushes down the corridor, past the cleaning lady, his eyes trained straight ahead.

I sink deeper still into the pillow, into the mattress. 'There's no plot, right?' I ask.

'Right,' Szibilla answers, and I feel my eyelids growing heavy, feel myself slowly drifting off.

'It's nice to hear you're doing alright.'

Those words again – they slice through the silence in my head; I wake. Szibilla is sitting exactly as before, eyes on the screen. Two men walk into a shop and explain in monotone voices that they'd like to sell some novelty items to help people to have fun. They present a mask they call 'Uncle One-Tooth'; one of the men puts it on. Baggy latex skin, grey hair, dead expression. Nobody laughs. The shop remains so quiet you could hear a pin drop; next scene. I doze off again.

At some point I hear a click and open my eyes. Szibilla has pressed pause.

'Half-time!' she says, bending to pick up a bottle of apple juice, which she holds aloft. 'Do you want some? It'll wake you up!'

Szibilla pours some into a short-stemmed wine glass and hands it to me. She puts the bottle to her lips. I drink half a glass and put it on the bedside table.

The film continues, one bizarre scene following another. Again, I fall into a doze. When I wake, something has changed. The laptop is shut, Szibilla is gone; my half-full glass of apple juice and the empty bottle are still on the nightstand.

'Szibilla?'

The main door is bolted from the inside, the key in the lock. The bathroom door is open, no light on. The door to the balcony is ajar. I step outside. Szibilla is sitting with her legs drawn up and a woollen blanket wrapped tightly around her body. I can see little more than her head.

'Everything alright?' I ask.

Her eyes are swollen, the lids puffier than usual. She draws the blanket more snugly around her. I go to stand next to her.

The first lights have come on in the valley below us, flickering as though in the wind. 'Old ghosts?' I ask.

Szibilla gives a nod.

On the other side of the Rhine, the Austrian mountains are a long-drawn wall, and above them is an expanse of slowly darkening sky.

'Is that the first time you've watched the film?' I ask.

'The third. The first time was at the cinema. With Nora.'

'Pretty depressing.'

'You think so?' Szibilla asks.

I move closer to the railing and look over it, to the right: the house at 122 Buchenstraße is impossible to see from here, it must be hidden by the few spruce trees at the base of the hotel.

'It's a shame Nora isn't here,' I say, turning to Szibilla. She looks up at me; there is something surprisingly gentle in her face.

'What are your plans for tomorrow?' she asks.

'I wanted to go back and see the old peat factory, as early as I can. Now that I can actually see again.'

'You wanted to take a look around?' Szibilla asks. 'Where you've come from, where you're going?'

'I really want to explore the building. Somehow I can't shake the feeling that it has a lot to do with me. With *my* old ghosts.'

Szibilla gazes back down into the valley.

'And what are your plans?' I ask.

'I'm meeting someone for breakfast at half past nine. Malita.'

'You two are becoming friends.'

Szibilla shifts in her chair, placing one foot after the other on the ground. 'Something is going to happen with Nora tomorrow,' she says, leaving my comment unremarked. 'I'm sure of it.'

'Meet you at lunchtime?' I ask.

'Yeah, sounds good.'

'Do you need anything else?'

Szibilla stands up, folds the fleecy blanket with a delicate shake, folds it again, and drapes it over the chair. 'No thank you,' she says. 'Good night.'

DAY FOUR

11 June

Romi

Five thirty in the morning, my feet move through the grass as though they've been treading this landscape all night long, down the hill, while the rest of me was lying in the hotel bed. Sleeping, resting. Sheep are grazing on the slope, bleating occasionally, and to the left, in the east, the outer rim of the sun is edging just above the mountaintops, although its rays have not yet penetrated through to me.

I walk quickly, slightly nauseous, but it's alright, it's bearable; I'm moving away from something, towards something, I'm in between. 'Things happen and they happen at the same time' – this light, this feeling, as on the morning after Leon's birth. The baby at my breast. Searching hands, searching mouth; and I wasn't quite there myself, I was still in transit, still the heavily pregnant woman who hours earlier had been walking straddle-legged through the rooms of her flat, keeping Phil within arm's reach – on the bed, on the sofa, at the kitchen table – and yet feeling utterly alone, utterly concentrated in that strange rush of pain, anticipation and forgetting; everything was internal, everything was external, there were no borders. A constant buzz, everywhere, and that downward pressure. Phil kept asking, 'Why don't we go to the hospital?' and I'd shake my head: I wanted to stay there, in my rooms, in our rooms, in that long-familiar flat. We stayed until the contractions set in, only then did we leave, Leon's head already half into the world, already crossing the border.

Until, finally, there he was. A plenitude that wrapped itself around his body, that went beyond it, that occupied the whole room; and yet the simultaneous, contrasting emptiness of my belly. As I stood under the hospital shower, I ran my hand over it again and again. It felt hollow, still an outward curve but without fixed content, an abandoned place, a place that would have to define itself once more. Yet this emptiness was forgotten the moment I was back in the room. I slid into bed, Leon on top of me, and my fingers traced his forehead, his cheeks, his neck; his skin, as if it were magic. He was already entirely a separate self, Leon, created from Phil and from me, between Phil and me; he breathed entirely by himself. Now there was a 'me' and a 'you', now there was a new 'us', and the borders between us and around us were new-drawn. Four years ago. A morning like this, only cooler.

And if Leon were to see me now, he would see a woman – nearly thirty years old or young – hurrying down a hill in the Rhine Valley, a bag over her shoulder and another new life in her belly. She has passed the pillarbox-red bench now, she has crossed a street, and if the woman noticed the child she would immediately break her silence, she would ask, 'What are you doing there, then?' She would pause, stroke the child's back and say, 'I have to go on, but don't worry, I'm here, I'm with you.'

The church tower is drawing nearer, five fifty-five. I walk down the street and reach the old town: cobblestones, everything asleep. The pharmacy is still closed, so are the bakery and the florist's; there are no signs out on the street, no advertising slogans to distract me. I take out my phone and open Google Maps, check the route again; then I go on, passing through an archway. On the other side is a larger street, already quite busy. I cross it. By now the sun has risen further.

Outside a school there is a square heaped with earth, as though a field were being built there; three men are flattening the area with rakes. They don't once raise their heads as I walk past. In a corner, near the fence: a hazel bush, but there's no Nora beneath it, or behind it either; no just-lit cigarette. I have found my rhythm, my pace. I walk alongside a canal and reach a train station underpass, then beyond that I find myself on a street of detached houses, among which is a stable. The front of it is studded with colourful plaques.

Industrial buildings appear in front of me: a transport company, a tool factory, a recycling centre; then a car park – that must be the one from yesterday. Not a single pedestrian, not one pedestrian in sight, but there are cars on the main road, which I have now reached. As if this were an integral part of the human condition, this sitting in a thing made of metal and an engine, this steering in any and all directions, this sense of freedom. Yet we are travelling on roads laid down for us, and the landscape on our left and right is inaccessible.

I cross the road. Now the landscape opens up before me: fields overgrown with grass, barns in the hazy light, rows of small trees. An excavator digging up the earth on the other side. The beginning of the Bannriet Reserve. My path leads straight ahead, the gravel crunching underneath my shoes. The picture of Nora hanging in her room appears in my mind's eye: she's on the banks of the Rhine, in a swimsuit. She's with her dad, but both of them are alone, both seem to be waiting for something, but what?

In the distance now I can see the hide from yesterday, and it feels to me as though it was an eternity ago that I sat here with Szibilla; another life, almost. Suddenly it feels like there is a fist knotted in my stomach, large and gradually trying to open. I stop, bend forward, wait for the pressure to subside, then I walk on, past the hide, a little slower now. The path curves. The old peat factory materialises in front of me, a wooden building made of different sheds. It is dark, a black hole. With every step I take towards the factory, the pressure in my stomach builds; I can't remember now why I wanted to come, I only know I did.

On my left, a long building flanks the edge of the path, some distance from the main building, its sides constructed out of loose boards. My eye falls through the cracks into the dark and then out again the other side, into the brightness of day.

Then, on my right, the main building begins. The path between the single shed on the left and the building on the right grows narrower, shadowy, so dark that I can't see a thing. It's as though the ground has been pulled out from under me, and for a second I find myself on the verge of freefall, into a space I don't know, a space below the earth, the space of the belly, my mother's belly, impossible to breathe; yet my legs are moving, I am taking steps, one, two, three, and eyes open. A new, old landscape appears before me: two small wooden wagons on rails, obviously long disused; a reed-encircled pond, and then beyond that, the expanse, again. I blink in the sun. It's as though a filter has been laid over my eyes: everything is drawn more clearly.

I walk in the direction of the pond. A grooved jetty extends two metres out into the water. I pass through the door-height opening that leads into the weathered steel cube, take ten steep steps down, and find myself in a small space below the level of the water, two metres by two. A narrow, vertical strip of Plexiglas offers a view into murky, greenish water, a softened, muddy bed. Stray bubbles of air break loose and rise to the waterline. Above the Plexiglas panel is a kind of horizontal shelf that guides the eye directly to the surface. The light mirrored in the water falls through the opening into this space, my space, onto the rust-red interior walls; swirling, shifting light; light in transit, in between, at once firm and fluid, visible and tangible. I sit down on the bench; half past seven. Again, I briefly doze.

Szibilla

The red carpet. The yellow dots. The pairs of shoes ambling across it. To the buffet, back. Everyone is eating. Talking over one another, or sitting in silence. My coffee is already cold. At the table next to mine is the family of three. The dad stares vacantly at his phone. The toddler is singing. Babbling something now and then. The dad repeats exactly what it says, but as a question. The mum keeps wandering from the buffet to the table. Back and forth. Something is always missing. Bread. Ham. Butter. Honey. Teaspoon. Another three-quarters of an hour, then I'm seeing Malita. By then I will have woken up. Let my brain get to work. The size of a pea, that's how it feels just now. I must have been dreaming.

The teenage girl from the first day is weaving through the tables. No giant of a dad, no Magic Flute of a mother. She's wearing a bum bag, and has a shrewd look in her eye. She is staring unabashed at people and their overloaded plates. At the backs of their bald heads. She is the only one in here with any sense. Now she's walking past the table where the pensioners are sitting. She walks more quickly. Disappears up the steps.

The young couple, they're here too. Today they have things to say to one another. They speak softly. Heads together. Lots of long-drawn pauses, in which she gazes at the bare tablecloth and he at the ceiling. She stirs her tea.

The neighbouring mum is asked by the dad to fetch the child

another poppy-seed roll. She stands up. Goes to the buffet. *All you can eat.* What a wonderful mantra.

I should get out of here. Go for a walk. Explore a bit, alone. I take my car keys. Walk past the buffet to the exit and out through the sliding door.

Romi

I sit up; I'm cold. I take my jumper out of my bag and put it on, gazing for a moment or two at the water, the way it moves. Then I call Dennis. A brief ring, and he picks up.

'Good morning,' I say.

I can feel his astonishment through the receiver; I can picture him in front of me, his hair sticking out in all directions, his eyes still full of sleep, questions, maybe. 'Romi!' is all he says, and I reply, 'I know, it's still early.'

'I've been awake for a while,' he says.

'How are you?'

Pause. He might be in bed with a book beside him; he might be at the window, looking out at the park in front of the house; he might be in the kitchen with a cup of black tea in his hand.

'Honestly, I feel like shit,' he says at last. 'You didn't call. You left me in the dark. It feels like you've pulled away from me.'

My bones are heavy, digging into the bench beneath me; I say, 'No. That wasn't my intention. I was overwhelmed.'

I stand up, take a few steps towards the panel, and crouch down in front of it. The tip of my nose is almost touching the Plexiglas.

'And what was so overwhelming?' Dennis asks.

A coot dives down into the green water, paddling towards the bottom with its feet, but turns back halfway.

'My fear,' I say. 'That everything is drifting apart. Slipping away from me.'

Dennis waits for a moment before he replies. 'You'll have to explain that a bit more.'

'If I focus everything on this, on what we have,' I say, 'then it's going to consume everything. Outshine everything. And I was afraid I'd feel as absent to Leon and the baby as my parents felt to me.'

Dennis is silent. Breathing.

'I think maybe I'm still a little scared,' I add.

'I don't really get it. How does fighting this help your children? Fighting against your emotions?'

Dennis's voice is harsh.

'It's not just something that happens to you, being in love,' I say. 'It's not as if you have no choice! It's also a decision. Being in love. And love itself.'

'Of course you have a choice,' Dennis says. 'At least, to an extent.'

'To what extent?'

'You can't choose to be in love,' he says. 'You can't consciously decide to love somebody, only not to. You can decide not to stay with someone you're in love with. You can decide not to be with me any more.'

'I know.'

'Doesn't sound like you care very much,' Dennis says.

'You think I don't care?' I ask back. 'Do you think I'm risking everything out of boredom?'

Dennis is quiet for a while.

'You know,' he says at last, 'the thought of losing you is unbearable. But what can I do?'

I stand up, lay my palm on the wall above the Plexiglas, where the light is swirling, and I ask, 'If love isn't an emotion, then what is it, in your mind?'

Dennis takes his time to answer; my hand wanders across the rough, cold Cor-Ten steel.

'I think love is different from being in love,' he says more calmly. 'Love is more all-embracing. Choosing not to love is definitely not a good idea.'

After a pause, he adds, 'The real question is how you live it.'

'Yes,' I say. 'And I can't deny that I'm afraid of getting hurt as well.'

I draw back my hand, sit down again on the bench.

'That I understand,' Dennis says.

I watch some air bubbles rise from the bottom of the pond to the water's surface and get caught there.

'I want this,' I say eventually. 'I want to be with you. Even if I don't know where it's going to take me.'

I hear Dennis exhale. 'There's nothing we can do about it,' he says, 'except to let go, to let it happen. And to see what comes. There's nothing I want more than for you to take that chance with me.'

The bubbles on the surface burst without a sound, one after another.

'You know,' I say, 'I wish I could find words for what this is. For what's happening. Inside me and between us and around us. But I can't find them, the words. Not the right ones.'

'So today words aren't good enough after all?' Dennis asks.

'What do you mean?'

'Maggie Nelson. *The Argonauts*. Didn't you say you'd read that book?'

'Ages ago.'

'I'm reading it right now. Maybe you remember the part about words being good enough, at least for Maggie Nelson,' Dennis says. 'Because what is inexpressible is always contained in the expressed.'

'Wittgenstein, right?' I say. 'It's a nice thought.'

'I think so too,' he says. 'And I share Nelson's opinion. The belief that words are good enough is why I write. Why I'm able to write at all. Because the only thing that wards off the fear of being unable to say anything is the certainty that the inexpressible is inherent in the expressed.'

'That all makes sense,' I say. 'Only – I'm not sure I believe it. I'd like to say more, to say the thing directly, to name it. But how?'

Dennis doesn't answer. He seems to be waiting for me to go on.

'Words are good enough for Maggie Nelson,' I say. 'Words aren't good enough for me. She writes about that too, doesn't she? I remember that quite well. That there's another way to look at it: by saying something concrete, everything else falls away, everything that is unnameable. It gets lost. Did you read it like that too?'

'Yes,' says Dennis.

'So if for example I say, "It's so nice to hear your voice today," what does that mean? It goes nowhere! It touches very little, virtually nothing. A die-cut sentence, just words, nothing behind them. What I really mean remains in the dark. But I' – I press my hand to my breastbone – 'I want to touch it!'

Silence. All that can be heard are the soft voices of the birds drifting through the gap into this space, my space; I hadn't noticed them before.

'Words are good enough. Words are not good enough,' Dennis said. 'Both thoughts are plausible, and clever. But ultimately, Nelson is talking about something else. The way I read it, at least. She's talking about the fact that the unnameable exists, flickering and fluid. And how much beauty there is in that.'

'That's probably the essence of it,' I say. 'And I do want to lose myself, you know, in the unnameable. In this labyrinth.'

I take a deep breath and say, 'I love you.'

'Like an Argonaut?' Dennis asks.

'Like an Argonaut,' I answer.

And then for a while we don't say anything, as more bubbles detach from the bed of the pond and a coot begins to chatter, and eventually I say, 'I'm leaving tomorrow. I'll call, okay?'

'Yes,' he says. 'Do that, please.'

I stay seated as I am, ringed in Cor-Ten steel, in reeds, in the pond behind the Plexiglas. My shirt forms wrinkles: hills exposed, shadowy troughs between them. I dig into my bag and take a sip of water. After a minute or two I rise and go up the stairs; each step makes a sound, each sound a little different in its resonance. No one to be seen, all as before, only even brighter now. The sun is already quite high.

On the other side of the track with the two wooden wagons is the old peat factory, this one building made up of many smaller buildings; it is a part of history. Part of the unnameable.

I walk up to it and step beneath a roof that links two sheds; it's dark. In the shed on the left, behind a barrier, is an old wooden wheelbarrow. Sandy floor beneath it. Blocks of peat stacked beside it: brick-size, brown as mud and crumbling. 'Former Peat Storage' I read on the informational placard on the wall. Here, too, light passes through the cracks, and here, too, dust has settled everywhere. On the other side, in the second shed: a conveyor belt also loaded with peat bricks, for demonstration purposes. I take a few steps back and am again under the open sky. On the exterior wall of the second shed is a short spiral staircase. I climb it and peer into the building. I have to get close to the window to see anything at all through the thick spiders' webs, but inside I can make out a large, dim room containing a single piece of equipment, a metre high and clearly long out of use: 'Peat Press'. Otherwise nothing. For decades, earth was dug up in this place, peat was cut, dried, loaded; for decades, it was the purpose of countless human beings to work here, to pass in and out of this building, and now how quiet it is, and it has nothing to do with me, and yet it does; even just that I am standing here and looking. History is like a bag of sand around my neck, a tiny hole in it from which the sand trickles down my back. It tingles; it is not my history, and still it is, like the history of my parents, my parents' parents.

I turn around. I'm still in the shade, but not far from my feet, at the bottom of the steps it is already sunny. Only now do I feel the pressure in my throat, upwards-travelling, slow, continuous; the pressure increases, grows warm, and now it's hard to breathe; but abruptly there is a release, and it feels like something is pouring out of my mouth. I look down at myself, but there is nothing, nothing visible. When I look back up, everything has widened: the colours, the shapes; the sun has nearly reached me – the light is already touching my toes. I fish out my phone and text Szibilla.

Hey there, how's it going? Still haven't heard from Nora. And you? Can you text me when you're heading back to the hotel? See you in a bit!

Szibilla

Earbuds in. Hands back on the wheel. I make a right turn. Drive up the hill. Now Romi picks up.

'Hello?' she says. Voice thick.

'Were you asleep?'

'Yes.'

'You didn't go for a walk?'

'I did. Got back about an hour ago, actually. What time is it?'

'Quarter to one,' I say. I take a bend without taking my foot off the pedal. 'Are you ready? We're going to see Nora.'

'You spoke to her?'

'I spoke to Anni on the phone.'

'Does Nora know we're coming?'

'Trust me,' I say, 'it's fine. I'll be at the hotel in a minute.'

Further uphill is the Beech Hotel. I roll down the window, rest my elbow in the gap. 'I'll wait for you outside,' I say. 'By the car.'

'Fine,' she says. 'I'll be right there.'

Anni

Nora is sitting on the desk chair by the window. Her legs are crossed, her gaze focused outside. Meret is perched in her lap, doing little hops. Clippety clop, clippety clop.

'Are you riding a horse?' Nora asks.

I glance at my watch. One of the gold-coloured stones on the dial is slightly tarnished. I'll have to take it in soon.

'I have to leave in five minutes,' I say. 'Or would you rather I stayed after all? If you've changed your mind, maybe? I could always call Dorothe and cry off!'

Nora turns her head to look at me. Meret stops bouncing. There is a dark stain on the carpet by the chair that wasn't there yesterday.

'Let me just quickly clean that up,' I say. I take a step into the hall.

'No!' says Nora, very loudly. I halt. 'Stay here!'

I go back into the room. Nora has turned slightly in her chair. Meret has slipped off her lap.

'I'll do it myself in a bit,' she says. Then she asks, 'Where are you going, anyway?'

Meret toddles over to the window. She reaches out her stubby arms and grabs on to the sill. She's obviously about to try to clamber up, so I hurry over. I'm standing very close to her now, and to Nora. Nora turns back to the window and lifts Meret onto her knees.

'We're doing three countries,' I say. Something has got snarled up in the hedge by the tomato greenhouse. A white plastic bag. I'd better get rid of that. In a minute.

'We're taking the coach to Bregenz then the cable car up the mountain for coffee and cake and a quick stroll. Then we'll have supper later on in Lindau.'

Nora says nothing. She puts her arms around Meret. She doesn't want me here.

'I won't be back before ten at the earliest,' I add.

Still, Nora doesn't say a word. The second hand makes five little leaps.

'Alright. Well give Dorethe my best,' Nora says.

Another five leaps of the second hand. I stroke Meret's cheek. She lets me. Like Nora did, when she was a girl. I bend down. 'Can Nanna have a kiss?' I ask.

She ducks away from me. I stand back up. I go to the door and turn back once more. 'Do you—' my voice breaks off. 'Do you have everything you need?'

Nora eyes me for a long time. She says, 'We'll be alright.'

Szibilla

I pull into the first free parking spot. Get out. The metal of the car is hot, I can feel the warmth of it at my back. I have the hotel entrance in my line of sight. Malita's breakfast in my stomach. The omelettes she made herself. The finely chopped parsley. Malita devoutly sprinkling some onto her omelette. Beatriz at the head of the table, silent most of the time – but it wasn't an awkward silence that she emanated. It was a calm, arising as from something self-contained. A letting-be. A no-longer-having-to. As if we were long-familiar spirits. And I wished then and there I could have lifted it away from Beatriz by some spell. The depression. The back pain. Malita was taciturn.

'Day-off mood,' she said.

The sliding door opens. It isn't Romi who emerges, it's a woman in hiking boots and a baseball cap, who makes straight for the hiking trails on the other side of the car park.

After a while Beatriz retired to her room. I went to stand by the wall, which was covered in dozens of pinned-up postcards. Beaches. Olive trees. Lighthouses. Seagulls. A city from above. There were Polaroids as well, and Malita was in nearly every one. Always with people. Always in high spirits.

'Everybody who comes here gets photographed,' Malita said.

She gestured to a Polaroid camera. Called in Beatriz, who came immediately to take a picture of us. Two, in fact. I can see Malita in my mind's eye. Pinning the first picture to the wall a moment later.

The hiker has decided on a route, and begins tramping off uphill. I reach into my trouser pocket. Take out the second picture. Almost identical to the first. Malita has one arm bent and her hand behind her head. She's looking sideways at me, slightly from above. Grinning. Her other hand behind my head. I'm looking into the camera as though afraid of something. But I felt good. Before the photograph, at least. And after.

'You look like such a scaredy cat!' Malita said. Said softly. Her voice reminded me of Nora. Where has Romi got to?

Romi

It's time. I'm queasy again, or still. I get dressed, leave the room behind me, head downstairs; I step outside into the heat, which is stronger all the time, or so it feels. There's Szibilla's car. She opens the driver's side door when she spots me and gets behind the wheel, sunglasses on her nose. I open the passenger door. Cold floods out of the interior; the air conditioning whirrs.

'Hi,' I say. 'Aren't we going to walk?'

'We'll have to go into the village later, most likely. Do some shopping.'

I slide into the passenger seat next to Szibilla and she starts the car. We drive the few hundred metres downhill in silence. Both the parking spaces outside Anni's house are free. We get out, walk through the garden, up the steps. Szibilla lifts the doormat and picks up a key. She unlocks the door.

'Looks like we've got the place to ourselves,' she says, unlacing her trainers and putting them on the shoe rack, one next to the other, the laces tucked into the shoe.

'Where's Anni?' I ask, slipping out of my sandals and taking three steps towards the living room. The floor is pleasantly cool.

'Off on some excursion with a bunch of other pensioners,' Szibilla says, bending down to pick up my sandals and placing them next to her shoes on the rack.

We step into the neatly ordered living room. Everything is in its place; even the floor is gleaming. There's a dummy on the coffee table, next to a single unlit candle. No sign of Nora.

We go back into the hall and up the stairs, and find ourselves standing again outside her childhood bedroom. I look at Szibilla, trying to catch her eye, to see if she's feeling the same way I am: like an intruder. But Szibilla is already knocking, and when nothing happens, she goes inside; I follow behind.

The room looks different from the last time. The shutters have been opened and the sunlight streams into the room, raising the temperature to baking. The air is stagnant. Even the cardboard boxes have been opened, their contents strewn across the floor; the objects form a trail leading from the boxes in the corner to the mattress where Nora is lying. The same tableau as three days earlier, only now Meret is lying there too. They both appear to be asleep. Szibilla and I walk slowly towards them. From close up I examine Nora's face in profile: she looks more relaxed, and she's gained a little colour. Her breathing is calm, her chest moving up and down.

'Nora?' I ask quietly. 'It's us.'

Nothing. Only Meret sighing in her sleep. Her little arms are stretched above her head, her face buried in Nora's chest.

I glance around the room. The two A4 photographs have been taken off the wall, the pins placed on the table, and in the bin underneath there are scraps of paper and aluminium foil, an empty bottle of juice, two notebooks. Szibilla points with one finger at the door. We go out and down the stairs, back into the living room.

'And now?' I ask, stopping in the middle of the room. 'What do we do?'

'We do the shopping. We cook.'

'You really think Nora won't mind?'

'No. But if it makes you feel better, I'll take full responsibility.'

She opens drawers, cupboards, the fridge, then turns to me and says firmly, 'Right, chicken soup!'

'Oh really, that's what you're going to make?' I ask. 'A childbed soup?'

'A what soup?'

'It's what the midwives recommend. Helps you to get your strength back after the birth.'

'Oh. Then yes, we're making Nora a childbed soup.'

We look up recipes on my phone and together we pick the first one that appears in the search results. I make a note: a stewing hen, carrots, celeriac, ginger, parsley root, coriander, cloves, juniper berries. 'There must be bay leaves and onions around here somewhere,' I say.

Szibilla points at a string of onions, then at the spice rack; all the jars are neatly labelled and look as though they've never seen a day's use. They're way to the right, the bay leaves. Suddenly it comes boring back, the nausea; that fist again in my stomach, like this morning. I fix my eyes on the square note on the table in front of me.

'You alright?'

'I feel sick. I think you'll have to cook without me.'

I straighten up, go to the sink, turn the water as cold as it will go and take a few gulps directly from the tap.

'Did Phil make it for you? Childbed soup?'

I turn off the tap. The water has frozen the fist, the nausea; or at least the notion of it helps.

'No,' I say. 'I ate a lot of pizza. And tons of pastries. I've never been so hungry as I was after Leon was born.'

Taking up the pen again. I jot on the list: biscuits, bread, butter. Then I open the kitchen window to let in a light waft of air. Szibilla takes the note out of my hand and says, 'Let's go.'

In the front hall I slip into my sandals. Szibilla kneels down on the floor and starts to lace her shoes; at that moment we hear a babbling, a whimper.

'We don't have a child seat, do we?' I ask.

'Not that I know of.'

We kick off our shoes again and go upstairs, into Nora's room. Meret is sitting upright on the mattress, rubbing her eyes. Nora is asleep.

'Hey, looks like somebody's awake!' I say, scooping her up.

Meret flails, thrashing her upper body back towards the mattress, but I hold her tightly and her resistance eases. She lets out one last wrathful noise, then lays her head on my chest exhausted, and after that there's not the slightest peep.

'Maybe you should do the shopping?' I say. 'And I'll stay here with Meret?'

'Yeah, let's do that,' Szibilla says, and with a nod to us, she leaves. I carry Meret through the house. Her heart against my chest, beating evenly, calmer by the minute. 'Would you like to play a game?' I ask.

Meret is silent.

'Maybe do a jigsaw puzzle?'

I stop in front of the kitchen window. A few cars pass up or down the street, motorbikes too, heavy machines. Across the street is the valley, the Bannriet Reserve.

'Out!' says Meret suddenly.

'You want to go into the garden?'

She's already halfway to the door, but she can't reach the handle; I follow, open it for her. One hand cautiously gripping the railing, she wavers for a moment. Then, hesitantly, she approaches the top step and takes it slowly, one leg following the other. Then another step, careful, precise; and in this manner she descends the stairs, step by step. I walk a short distance behind her. When she reaches the bottom she turns to me, claps both hands and laughs, happy and proud, beaming with her whole face. Then she bounds across the lawn as fast as she can on her short legs, towards the vegetable patch, where Anni is growing lettuce, courgettes, chard. She pokes a finger into the soil, then digs in with one hand and with the other.

'Worm, where, where worm?'

I join her in digging, my hands gliding easily through the loose soil, which is damp and black, must be freshly watered; I'm feeling better here, here I'm not so sick, despite the heat. I dig until I find an earthworm, grasp it with two fingers and hold it aloft. Meret is jubilant, peering closely at the way the worm curls and twists, inspecting its lustrous skin, the fluid transitions of its colours: brown, orange, black. She holds out her hand. I let the worm slip into her palm and she recoils; the worm falls to the ground and seeks a way back in; already it has disappeared.

'Again!' cries Meret.

We dig on, in the places that have not been planted, and find two more worms, observe them, let them crawl back into their earthen kingdom; and it feels to me as though Leon were here too, as though he too were digging, his hands already larger than Meret's, his thirst for knowledge vast. I see him standing in our garden, pointing out the individual plants. 'What's that?' he asks. 'And that?', 'And what's that called, Mama?', and I answer as best I can, trying to skirt the gaps in my knowledge; Leon's small face, his gentle eyes, his soft hand which he tucks into mine – not often, but when he does, he does so firmly.

We can't find any more worms now, and Meret is thirsty. We return to the house, and as I walk into the living room, I'm suddenly struck by the thought that Nora grew up here, that she brought all these rooms to life, made them her own; that this is the place where she made her first discoveries, had her first disappointments; that this is the place that shaped her, this gleaming house with its marble dining table, its big TV and heavy rug in front of it; this place with all its frills and frippery: the bowl of colourful sand and candles, the clowns and angels made of porcelain. What did it look like when Nora was younger, a child like Meret; what has changed? I'm seized by the urge to go upstairs and ask, to ask all the questions for which I have no answers. I pass Meret the bottle and she sucks on it greedily. Outside, a car door slams, and moments later Szibilla is in the hall. She has a paper bag from the supermarket in her right hand and a large melon balanced in her left.

Szibilla

The cold water runs over the chicken. Pink skin, faintly pimpled. Odious. But today it is important. It must restore Nora's strength.

I switch off the tap and deposit the stewing hen onto a clean plate. Bend down. There, here's a pot that's big enough. I put the chicken inside. Fill it up until the water is five centimetres below the rim. I turn on the stove. Wash the vegetables. Pick up the knife. Chop the celeriac, ginger and carrots into fine pieces. I halve the onion and put it onto the aluminium foil, then onto the smallest hob. I can hear Meret in the living room. She's crying. Screeching. I wait until the onion is black then take it off the stove. Skim the foam off the chicken. Set the timer. Thirty minutes. Then I go into the other room. Meret is red in the face. Romi is standing beside her.

'No idea what's the matter with her,' Romi says. 'She wants the dummy, but every time I give it to her, she throws it away.'

I wipe my hands on my trousers. Crouch down. Meret stares at me, disconcerted.

'Hello,' I say. 'Why don't we have a little read of a book?'

Instantly Meret makes a beeline for the television, where there are a couple of children's books on the shelf below. She points at the fattest. *My First Fairy Tales*. I sit down on the sofa, and Meret sits next to me. On the cover of the book is a princess. Blonde, blue dress. The prince is kneeling in front of her. A boy in a red robe. Red cap. Two feathers in it.

'Which one would you like to hear?' I ask, opening the book. I skim the table of contents. Little Red Riding Hood. Sleeping Beauty. Old Mother Frost. Snow White. Rumpelstiltskin. Cinderella.

'All of them,' Meret says.

And so I start from the beginning.

Romi

I go upstairs and open the door to Nora's room. She's lying on her back, legs bent, eyes open.

'Nora!' I say, astonished.

I want to go to her, give her a hug, but instead I hover in the doorway. Nora nods towards the window and says, 'It's really fucking hot in here!'

Then she flips onto her side: back to me, face to the window.

'Shall I get you something to drink?' I ask.

'No thanks,' she says. 'Where's Meret?'

'Downstairs, with Szibilla.'

I close the door behind me and sit cross-legged on the floor; the position increases the pressure on my belly, but I stay there anyway. My knee is touching the edge of Nora's mattress; there are worlds between us. Nora's reddish hair is greasy. The pillow under her head is dotted with tiny flakes of skin.

'How are you feeling?' I ask after a while.

No reply.

The trail between the cardboard boxes and the mattress has changed. Objects have been moved closer to Nora: two photo albums, a few loose pictures, and there, next to her head, is an open diary, the pages full of writing, a spidery scrawl that's obviously hers.

'I don't know what to say,' I tell her. 'I really want to give you something.'

Slowly Nora rolls onto her back. There's a slight tear in the middle of her bottom lip. Her skin is waxy.

'Were you looking for something specific in the boxes?' I ask.

She makes a dark noise, something between a laugh and a sigh. I stretch out my legs along the mattress, putting the right one over the left: better.

'What's that smell?' Nora asks. 'Is my mother back?'

'Szibilla is cooking,' I say. 'I know. We should have asked instead of just showing up like this.'

'It's fine.'

Nora is looking at the ceiling; she appears to be searching for something in the patterns, new ciphers, perhaps, or figures; a previously unrecognised clue. Then she turns her head towards me and examines me like the ceiling. She reaches out her arm and puts a hand on my belly, just very briefly; then she pulls herself swiftly up and covers the few steps to the window, pausing in front of it, knees braced. She tilts it open. She's wearing a white T-shirt printed with a child's drawing over her shorts: a piggy bank and golden coins flying around the pig. She lets herself slide down until she's leaning against the wall underneath the window, then there she sits, her face unusually grave.

'Shall we go downstairs? Find Meret and Szibilla?' I ask.

Nora plucks at her T-shirt with two fingers, exactly on the picture of the pig, then lifts it up and fans it; out of nowhere she says, 'You haven't spent much time outside the last couple of days. You're so pale.'

Her eyes twitch twice, as though she's trying to stop herself from blinking.

'Szibilla showed me Bannriet,' I say.

Nora strokes her palms over her face; she seems calmer now.

'What on earth are you wearing?' I ask.

Nora glances down at herself. There is a strip of brown along her hairline, more than two centimetres wide: her natural hair colour, which I haven't seen for a long time.

'It's from when I was at school,' she says. 'I drew it for some competition for the bank. Then they printed all the designs on a giant T-shirt for the kids who entered. Such a dumb idea. The nineties, man. These days they hand out stuffed monkeys with cute little faces. Luring in customers even earlier.'

'Have they tried that on with Meret yet?'

'Probably,' says Nora. Pushing herself up off the floor, she gets to her feet. 'I want to go back to sleep,' she says, returning to the mattress to sit down.

'Do you mind if I stay?' I ask. 'With you?'

Nora shakes her head, throws back the cotton blanket and slumps onto the mattress again. I lie down, also on my back, in the bed which smells of sleep, of Nora's old clothes, and something else, something sweetish. Our bodies are touching only along our forearms, as sweat slowly forms between them, gluing us together. It's like it used to be, when we'd go whirling across the dance floor, never searching for a man but always for each other, and sharing a drink at the bar, exhausted, side by side.

'It's been way too long,' I say.

'Since what?'

'Since we went dancing.'

She seems to be falling back to sleep.

I roll onto my side. My eyes fall on an open photo album on the floor. I tug it a little closer to me. One of the pictures is of a child, Nora, ten years old, let's say, in fancy dress: Nora as a little witch. She's wearing a patchwork skirt that makes her twice as wide and reaches to the floor, her eyes are lined thickly in black, and a neon-green scarf is tied around her head. Where the hair is visible, poking out of the scarf, it's tousled. She's leaning on a walking stick, although not really putting any weight on it, and giving the camera a surly stare. Nora is elegant in a very specific way. How beautiful she is.

Beside me, she moves. She sits up, and for a moment she leans over the same photo album, then closes it, stands, and puts it into one of the cardboard boxes.

'Let's go downstairs,' she says, more to herself than to me, as she bends down to pick up the rest of the photo albums and diaries and tosses them carelessly into the boxes, one after another. Lid on. Then, without warning, she turns to me and asks, 'Are you looking forward to having that baby?'

I run my fingers through my hair, caught off guard, and suddenly I feel very grimy.

'Hey,' I say, 'do you mind if I take a shower?'

'Is that your answer?' Nora asks, then waits a couple of seconds before she goes on. 'Ah, Romi. What have we done with our lives? And what do we have still in store for us?'

She stands before me, arms dangling, and her questions – which were barely even framed as such – take up all the space, making the room even narrower, even smaller.

'There are wonderful things in store for us!' I say. 'I'm sure of it. And in fifty years we'll be sitting out on a terrace we built ourselves somewhere, telling each other dirty stories and drinking apricot liqueur.' Nora stands where she is, lost in thought; I walk up to her and hug her, feel her narrow back, her ribcage, graceful but strong. Nora puts her arms around me too.

After a while we let go, and Nora leaves the room. A wave of nausea comes over me. I squat down, breathe in, breathe out; a towel comes flying and I catch it.

'Use whatever you need in the bathroom. I'll be downstairs.'

I flush the toilet and stand under the shower. The hanging shelf is full of expensive-looking products. I let the water run over my body; a firm, abrasive stream. The water splashes onto the floor, collects, gurgles down the drain. I lather up with the smallest possible amount of shampoo, trying not to breathe so the artificial fragrances don't make me feel even worse, and rinse everything off. There remains a pleasant film on my skin, a tingling sensation; I dry off, but the sensation lingers. I put my clothes back on and go down to the living room.

Nora is sitting on the sofa, Meret in her arms; Nora's feet are on the coffee table in front of her, and between the tabletop and her feet is the storybook. Her eyes are closed, her head resting on the sofa. Szibilla is bustling in the kitchen: cutlery jangles, a drawer is closed, the extractor fan is turned up a notch.

I sit down in the armchair diagonally across from Nora and Meret. The TV is mounted on the opposite wall, the black screen reflecting us as we sit motionless.

Eventually Meret removes herself from her mother's lap and walks purposefully towards the vitrine containing the glasses. She opens the door and begins to clear them out. I go over, pick her up.

'Come on, let's find something else for you to do,' I say.

There is an empty biscuit tin on the shelf, which I fill with objects I find: two light gloves, animals made of felt, tissues which I pull out of the pack and place in the tin. Meret immediately starts taking things in and out of the tin, the felted animals in the glove, the glove on her head. She chuckles contentedly, and all at once a sentence pops into my head, a quotation from Susan Sontag this time: 'It adds to people's consciousness and makes things more complicated, which I think is always good.'

Szibilla emerges from the kitchen and flops down on the sofa next to Nora.

'Those are for you,' she says, nodding in the direction of the table. I follow her gaze and see an orange tin. Ginger pastilles.

'I found them in the kitchen. Good for nausea,' she adds.

I take three pastilles out of the tin and put them in my mouth; spiced and sweet. I suck, and meanwhile Nora slowly takes one foot after the other off the book of fairy tales. Immediately Meret ambles over and points at the book. 'Look!'

Nora eyes it briefly and asks, turning to Szibilla, 'Is that what you were reading to her?'

'Cover to cover.'

She examines the book again as though she finds it repugnant, then stands up and puts it on the very top shelf; I nudge the remaining bits of pastille between my back teeth and my cheek. Nora turns back to us. Something in her face has changed.

'I've got something else for you, something better,' she says. 'The myth of Baubo!'

Nora sits back down on the sofa, back straight as a die.

'I already know that one,' I say.

'Only the bowdlerised version!' Nora replies.

Szibilla murmurs something, vanishes into the kitchen and returns. 'We'll eat after this,' she says, slumping back onto the cushions.

Nora nods. 'Yep, fine,' she says, 'but just listen to me now, alright?'

How different Nora seems. How animated, her hands underscoring everything she says; she's speaking more rapidly than before.

'Demeter had a daughter, Persephone. Persephone liked to wear wellies and corduroy waistcoats from morning till night, because of course she had work to do in the fields and in the forests. That was where she liked to spend her time, and she could find nearly all the things she needed there. She preferred to be alone most of the time anyway, and when she did feel like seeing people, she would invite them round, and her parties were always uproarious. One day, she caught the attention of Hades. He saw her hair, of which he said, "It's beautiful," and her face, which he described the same way, and her little house he also saw. It wasn't very big but it was the most ostentatious in the whole town, painted a bilious green that glowed in the night. Hades thought, *I need her, Persephone, somehow I have to tame her.* And he said to his brother, Persephone's dad, this guy called Zeus, something like, "I've fallen in love." At first Hades tried to talk her round. He tried to show himself to best advantage, but she wanted nothing to do with him or his Underworld, which he pretended was one big fabulous party. So Hades made up his mind to kidnap her, and even her father, the so-called Father of the Gods, condoned his plan. Tacitly, of course. Hades came at night and took her from her house. Persephone fought back, she called for help, but no one heard. The next day, when she went to visit, Demeter realised that Persephone was missing. She knew at once that something was very wrong, and searched for her daughter in all her favourite places – in the field, near the wood-shed – but she had vanished without trace. Demeter continued to search everywhere. The towns at first, but then she strayed far into the countryside. She cursed everything, allowed the plants to wither and the earth to dry. Nothing grew or flourished any more, everything was barren and lifeless, no more children were born. Everything wasted away. Suddenly, she realised where Persephone must be. The Underworld! It had to be. But Demeter had no idea how to get her out. Just then, another goddess pulled up in her convertible. Baubo, a wizened figure with a belly that was also her head and eyes that were also her breasts. She stopped next to Demeter. "Hey you!" she yelled. "What are you looking for?" Demeter walked on as if in a delirium, paying no attention to Baubo. "Hey, sister, can you hear me?" Baubo asked. She drove right up to Demeter and honked the horn three times, and now Demeter turned to look. Baubo began to swing her breasts. "Hey, look!" she said, jumping out of the car and lifting up her skirt. She showed Demeter her large, fleshy, pink-and-brown, magnificently beautiful vulva. When Demeter saw, she stopped and started to laugh. The laughter solved everything. The curse was broken. In an instant Demeter felt better, and the plants began to sprout again.'

Nora pauses for a moment, taking a deep breath. For a second I'm not sure if she's going to go on or not. Meret slaps her hands against the floor and on the tin, which rattles. Then she tries to put the glove on like a sock, she looks at Nora, then concentrates on her game again, and Nora continues her story. 'And now Demeter marched straight down to the Underworld. She left Charon in the dust, swam across the River Styx, and ordered

Hades to release her daughter. No luck. Hades claimed, well, he claimed that Persephone had foolishly eaten four pomegranate seeds, which meant of course that she could never leave the Underworld, and she would have to stay. "What sort of drivel is that?" Demeter said. "Persephone is coming home. Now."

'"Okay," said Hades, "since it was only four pomegranate seeds, I'll make you a deal. Persephone will stay down here with me for four months out of the year, and for the remaining eight months she can live up there with you, in the sun." Demeter took two glasses and a bottle of ouzo out of her bag and handed one of them to Hades. "Have a drink," she said, "it'll do you good." She poured one for him and one for herself, and after three or four glasses Hades was feeling a lot more relaxed. He sank to the ground, playing with one of his nipples, and asked Demeter if she would pamper him a little. Demeter put one foot on his stomach – that was a no – and she could have squashed Hades with her bare sole, but there was no need, he was already asleep. Demeter fetched Persephone. Baubo was waiting for them on the other side of the Styx, and together they returned home. No one could have failed to hear Baubo's shrieks of joy – really, no one. At most they could be ignored. She took Demeter and Persephone home and then drove off on new adventures. Demeter and Persephone, on the other hand, changed their names, and if they didn't die, then they're still alive today.'

Short silence. Nora's expectant face, her eyes flicking from Szibilla's to mine and back. Szibilla raises an invisible glass.

'Cheers!' she says. 'To your version of the Persephone myth!'

Nora raises an invisible glass of her own, but mid-gesture she lets her hand drop. It lands on her thigh; she slumps back against

the arm of the sofa. 'In real life Persephone had a son, you know,'
Szibilla says.

'What's "real life" when you're talking about a myth?' Nora
retorts. 'And anyway, in "real life" Zeus wasn't just Persephone's
father but the father of her son as well. Lovely, eh? I'm taking
the liberty of rewriting it.'

She sits back up. 'Obviously you can still read all those myths
about powerful men and downtrodden women, they're everywhere, and there's probably minimal variation. But you can read
other books as well, you know. Ones about how myths even
older than the story of Persephone were overwritten. About how
goddesses were scratched out of history in favour of a bunch of
silver-tongued male gods. I could give you countless examples!'

'Nora, I'm familiar with them,' Szibilla says.

'Xiwangmu, Cybele, al-Uzza – they were goddesses without
a male supporting cast. In those days male dominance wasn't a
thing!' Nora says, explaining anyway, still on edge.

'Or Eve!' she says. 'As though the story as it's mostly told
today is the only possible variant. In fact, in the very earliest
tellings, Eve and Adam were created together. As equals! No ribs,
nothing about any hierarchy. We have to rethink everything,
everything, not just the Persephone myth. It's probably too
difficult for us to even imagine the extent to which these stories
have shaped us. Stories that keep women down – that emerged
out of fear!'

Meret is banging the flat of her hands against the outside of
the vitrine. Nora picks her up and pulls her back onto her lap.

'What names did they choose, Demeter and Persephone?'
I ask.

'Call them whatever you like,' answers Nora immediately.
'A and B. Alma and Berta. Szibilla and Romi. Vulva and vagina.
It's an ancient custom, displaying your vagina like that, did you
know? They were celebrated all across the planet! The vulva and
vagina, the gateway to the world.'

Szibilla gets up and heads into the kitchen. I look out of the
window. Clouds have gathered, sharply contoured on one side
and vague on the other.

'It's strange that I find it strange,' I say. 'The thought of showing you my vulva.'

'Why?' Nora asks.

'You can't even imagine the amount of shame I carry around
with me.'

'Trust me,' Nora says, 'I can.'

'You?' I ask. 'You're shamelessness incarnate!'

'If you only knew,' Nora says. And after a few seconds she
goes on: 'It might sound profane, all that vulva stuff, but it isn't.
It's no coincidence that so many women get the size of their
labia reduced. It's everything pushing them to do it. Pictures,
all the examples they see. It's so important, I think, to show our
daughters the variety of vulvas that exist. To tell them: this part
of the body looks as individual as a stomach, a knee, a back. We
desperately need little girls to see it earlier, to see how many different shapes and sizes there are, the range of beauty! The same
way that they should be hearing a range of stories.'

Nora leans in a little closer, as though afraid I'm not hearing
her properly.

'My mother never talked to me about any of it. She just did
what she did and never reflected on it. After my dad left, she

stumbled from one man to the next. None of them treated her well, and in the end they all walked out. But she still cried her eyes out when they did.'

'I don't think I quite understand what those two things have to do with each other,' I say.

'It's so important to really consider history. The stories. And the things we're dependent on. We have to try and understand them so that we don't fall prey to them, so that we can reposition ourselves.'

Meret toddles towards Nora, who scoops her up into her lap again, but Meret doesn't want to sit, she wants to stand on her mother's thighs.

'Was it psychological or physical abuse your mother experienced?' I ask.

Now Meret plops down, belly to belly with Nora, and she keeps reaching into the sleeves of Nora's T-shirt.

'Hard to say for sure.'

'What about your dad, what was he like?'

'Imagine Emrik times two but minus the drugs,' she says. Nora grasps Meret's hand without taking her eyes off me and says, 'Now it's our turn.'

'What?' calls Szibilla from the kitchen. 'Are you still on the same topic?'

'Yes!' Nora shouts back. 'We need to talk! About our vulvas, our cunts, our pussies, about ourselves in this world! And by "us" I mean you and me and Baubo, and I mean all women, and every other creature under the sun! We need to talk about the shame that makes so many things impossible!'

Szibilla appears in the doorframe. 'Sure, but not right now,' she says. 'Time to eat.'

Szibilla

Soup ladle in the pot. Soup into the bowls. Bits of vegetable. Shreds of chicken. The lovely fat. It will give her strength. Nora is already spooning it up.

I dip Meret's child-size spoon into her soup. Blow. She opens her mouth. Slowly, I put in the spoon. She swallows.

'Delicious,' Romi says. 'You can feel it doing you good.'

Nora has already half finished her bowl. I stand up. Over by the sink, I slice a lemon in two.

'Is there a lemon press anywhere around here?' I ask.

Nora shrugs. 'How would I know?'

I sit back down. Squeeze the lemon with my hand. The droplets land in my bowl.

'Would you like some?' I ask them. They both nod. I let the juice drip into their soups. Then I lick the squeezed lemon, biting out the flesh. I take it to the compost bin and let it drop.

'Since when are you so into lemons?' Nora asks.

'They help me keep a cool head,' I say. I slice a second lemon and bring it to my seat.

Nora pushes away her empty bowl. That's all she can take for now, she says, and tells us she's going back upstairs to lie down.

She gives Meret a kiss on the forehead, then leaves. The child watches her go.

'What did you think of the film yesterday, by the way?' I ask Romi. 'Apart from it being depressing.'

She puts a spoonful of soup into her mouth. Thinks. Then she says, 'I don't feel like I really got it.'

'You slept through most of it.'

She puts the spoon down and asks, 'Anyway, shouldn't we be heading off in a bit?'

'Yeah. As soon as Nora is awake again.'

Meret's eyes are fixed on me. She doesn't miss a thing.

'Nanna where?' she asks.

I take a cloth and wipe the soup off her face. 'Nanna called a little while ago, asking how little Meret was doing.'

'Did she want anything else?' Romi asks.

'No. She was just asking if we were getting on alright. Without her.'

I turn back to Meret. 'Nanna's off on a little hike. And the two of us are going out soon as well.'

Romi helps herself to another half a ladle. Asks, 'Do you have any ideas about where we could go?'

'Anni told me where the child seat is. We'll go for a drive somewhere. Somewhere high up.'

Meret wants to get down. Romi wrings out the cloth in the sink and cleans off the girl's hands. Meret wobbles off towards the living room. Reaches for the remote control.

'Have you been thinking about what's next for Nora too?' Romi asks.

'Now, you mean? Or in the future?'

'Both.'

'One step at a time. She'll find her way.'

Romi eats a little more. Her lips are glistening with oil. She looks up.

'That film yesterday, Szibilla. What's its significance for you?' she asks. She takes the pepper mill, twists it. Pepper trickles down into her bowl.

'It's a work of art,' I say. 'Every single scene is perfectly arranged. Every single glass. Every shoe. In the right place. Every word. Every gesture. Everything has been thought through. Every camera angle creates a tableau, and each tableau is followed by the next. More than that – each one builds on the last.'

Romi frowns. She mashes a cube of vegetable with her spoon.

'But it's also pretty fucking difficult, as a whole,' she says.

'Andersson is trying to depict human beings as they really are,' I say. 'I find them restful, those images, because they're so self-contained. Keeps the rest of the world out. All the bullshit. It stays outside. For once.'

Romi puts on a voice, higher pitched. 'It's nice to hear you're doing alright.'

I pull a face. 'As Uncle One-Tooth would remark, rarely is that the case.'

Romi gives a brief laugh. 'I guess it's just not my sense of humour.'

'I loved it,' I say. 'The sarcasm. Always have.'

Romi puts her bowl on top of Nora's. Carries both to the sink.

Romi

I lie down on the sofa in the living room, alone; it's a good thing, this small solitude. I hear Szibilla packing things for Meret. I stretch out, leaf through the children's books still lying around. A text from Phil.

> *Finally tidying up! (We're really glad you're coming home tomorrow.)*
> *Leon & Phil*

Plus a photo of Leon in the front room, his back leant against the wall beside a bookcase – they must have just put it up. The silvery shelves are empty bar a single book. When I zoom in, I read the title: *1Q84*, Haruki Murakami.

Leon's gaze seems to pass through the lens, his eyes presumably fixed on Phil, who is taking the picture; those bright eyes, both Phil's and Leon's: so familiar. I put another ginger pastille into my mouth. 7 p.m. I take out my notebook.

NOTE

IT COULD GO LIKE THIS

I stay here in the Rhine Valley, I give birth to the child somewhere in the forest, with Baubo's help, and simply lie here in the green and wait until the child is big enough to move on, to take a new path, a very different one.

IT COULD GO LIKE THIS II

I travel to Japan, I gaze out over the cliff and there remain, I put down roots and grow for eight hundred years. And if a child comes to sit beneath me, leans against my trunk, then I begin to pulse, very softly, knock, knock; 'I've been waiting here, waiting for you.'

IT COULD GO LIKE THIS III

I throw in my lot with Nora, we live together with our children in a house, like sisters, a family, and Szibilla visits every Sunday, bringing soup and wine.

IT WILL GO LIKE THIS I

I go back to Phil and Leon, and to Dennis; and back also means: forward. Back means: on. On means: continuing to negotiate those spaces, to feel out where the borders lie and to uphold them.

IT WILL GO LIKE THIS II

I look for a room all of my own, I write.
I write:

IT COULD GO LIKE THIS IV

We take it even further: we dissolve it – household, ownership, exclusivity – we dissolve it all with words and gestures. We try, we try at least.

Nora comes downstairs with a rucksack; she goes into the kitchen, and I hear her switch the kettle on. After a while she comes back out, crosses through the living room to open the front door.

Outside, Szibilla is holding the garden hose. The jet of water shoots aloft and fans, landing two metres or so before her on the lawn. Meret is careening in circles around her, passing under the water again and again; she's drenched. For a moment or two she doesn't notice Nora in the doorway, but when she does she bolts straight towards her and wraps her arms around her legs.

'Oof, you're cold!' says Nora, lifting Meret high into the air, pressing her close. 'Let's get you into something dry, then we'll set off.'

Nora turns to me. 'You coming?'

Szibilla

Bends. All bodies shunted to the same side. Sometimes left. Sometimes right. These forces to which we surrender ourselves. The force of gravity. Centripetal force.

'Could you maybe slow down a bit, please?' Romi asks from the back seat.

I ease my foot off the pedal. Take a left turn at the roundabout in the village. We're passing houses. A second-hand clothing shop. A pizzeria. A butcher's. A Lidl. A Leica office. Another roundabout. Then the next village. The same picture. Nearly. After the third village, the turn-off. Now the road is climbing. We're driving upward. Past the restaurant. Fifty metres to go. Then I park the car at the edge of a field.

'Meret is asleep,' Nora says.

She lifts the child gently out of the car seat. Limp. And heavy. Romi carries the rucksack and I bring the bag of wood. We walk across the field towards the fire pit at the top of the small rise. The panorama opens up before us. The Rhine Valley. Lake Constance. Nora places Meret on her jacket in the grass. Freshly mown. I cover her with a fleece blanket. Romi and Nora sit down on the bench that someone's put here.

Romi

Crackling, rustling; the sky has darkened in the distance, at the far end of the valley where it stretches towards the south.

The sky above us is still unclouded, and it's clear where the Rhine flows into Lake Constance too, above the whole lake, in fact. Yet the air has cooled. Szibilla throws on more wood, and immediately the logs catch light. Nora takes three enamel cups out of the bag, pours water over the teabags, laughs and holds out two of the cups to Szibilla.

'*Love is where compassion prevails and kindness rules* or *The first word you utter must identify you?*'

'Are you trying to tell me something?' Szibilla asks.

'Yogi is. Through their tea.' Nora turns one of the labels towards Szibilla. 'Here, take this one.'

'It's much too hot,' Szibilla says. 'For tea.'

'But not for a fire?' Nora asks, although it must be obvious to her, more obvious even than it is to me, how much Szibilla loves fire. You can tell from the meticulous arrangement of the small sticks of wood, the almost ceremonial fashion in which she struck the kindling aflame. The way she lit a small fire, then gradually placed the bigger logs on top.

Nora hands me the second cup.

'It's going to rain soon,' she says.

'Is that what it says on my tea?'

'You're getting the one about the first word.'

Nora leans over Meret to check her temperature, then takes

her own cup and sits back down beside me. Szibilla has already set her cup down next to the bench and is gazing into the flames.

The lake looks like a carpet, a hovering blue, stray patches of silver in the last reflected light; all the sailboats are gone now, there are no ships; the gale warning lights are already flashing to their own rhythm; orange lights are going on and off all around the lake.

Szibilla

Hot air around us. From time to time, a layer of cool washes in between. Romi is sipping her tea. Nora is leaning against her. Both are staring straight ahead. Into the landscape.

'What does your tea label say?' I ask Nora.

'Be cosmic not cosmetic,' she replies. Without moving her head. We puff and blow, the three of us. Meret murmurs something in her sleep. I bend over her. A gust of wind flicks a corner of the blanket upwards. I tuck it tight.

They're approaching. More quickly now. The dark clouds. The storm. They're going to get more frequent. In the future. Longer and longer heatwaves. More and more powerful storms in their wake. Gales. Floods. The fire in front of me continues to burn. Undaunted. Unbridled light. Such seeming contrast. Sparks fly up into the air, thrown high. They burn out and they are gone. A clap of thunder. The first heavy drops. The rain will wrench open the fields, the unpaved roads.

'We should go,' I say. 'It'll be a deluge soon.'

Romi

It's dark — how quickly it happened; the fire is still crackling.
Szibilla shakes out the last splashes of water over it and stamps
out the embers with a log, as if that were needed now. I don't
want to go. I'd like to feel this: the wind, the rain. Meret is in
Nora's arms; she's woken now. We trudge back across the field
to the car. The raindrops are getting bigger, the wind whips our
hair and nearly tears the clothes from our bodies. For a moment
all we can do is stand, to plant ourselves against it, against the
squall, this wild business, and in this moment I could fly away,
I could watch all of it unfold from higher up; but we stumble on
to the car, fling open the doors and clamber in as quickly as we
can. Szibilla starts the engine, but suddenly the rain is coming
down like crazy, it's drumming on the roof and against the windows, and we sit, motionless. I try to say something, but I can't
even hear myself; Szibilla turns on the interior lights and I see
Meret's frightened face clutched to Nora's chest. Nora turns her
eyes to mine, motioning with her hand as though to say: We're
not getting out of here.

Epilogue

QUESTIONNAIRE FOR NORA AND SZIBILLA / ON SHAME

(What I'd like to say to you / What I have never told anybody so directly / What I have never asked anybody so directly / Ask me why.)

Do you remember when you were four or five years old? If yes, what did you want to be, what did you dream of? And what did you love? What is your earliest memory, and who figures in it?

Are many of your childhood memories bound up with your parents, and if no, then with whom?

Are there words you don't utter because you don't have the courage? Are there things that you would like to say one day, loud and clear, to someone else, or simply to yourself?

And as a child, were you able to express everything you wanted to, or did you endure it too, that great familial silence? Or did you simply ignore the silence and speak anyway, speak freely?

At what point did you realise that you were 'a girl'? That you would become 'a woman'? And what did that mean to you?

Did you too have a phase when you were astonished by the size of your genitals? For a while I felt like they wouldn't stop growing, and eventually I thought: This is never going to stop, my lips are getting longer and longer, they are turning into fans that will eventually outgrow me, envelop me completely; and from the outside I will be nothing but vulva, and the tiny human on the inside will be almost impossible to make out. *The problem: at the time I had no word for it, for the vulva, and that meant I would have become nothing. (You gave me that word, Nora, did you know that?)*

When puberty began, did you too examine in great detail the glistening thighs of the women in fashion magazines, the large, firm breasts? Did you simply accept it, this polished beauty, did you also think: this is how they look, men, women – this is how one ought to look? And were you also shocked, then, upon examining yourself shortly before your first period? Were you alarmed to see your body abruptly round and huge, not the vulva only but your hips, your belly, upper arms and thighs as well? Only your breasts were too small! I remember the first rolls of flesh and the first fissures in my skin: one morning I discovered the stripes on my thighs, one on the left and one on the right. I tried to wash them off, rub them away, but they wouldn't go away – in fact they spawned others, more and more of them, turning silver over time.

Did your mother, too, cycle on and off a diet? Did you know countless girls trying to lose weight who suffered from bulimia or drank only fruit tea with sweetener and claimed they did it to be healthy?

Szibilla, what kind of woman do you want to be, and Nora, what woman and what mother?

Memories come to me. The period, for instance, when I almost completely stopped going to the swimming pool. I didn't want to lie around in a bikini any more, I didn't want those eyes on me or people knowing that I do not glisten, am not polished, that my hips are streaked, my body sluggish. When I did go I stayed in the shadow, wrapped myself in a towel and said I didn't like swimming, and no, I wasn't in the mood, and no, I wasn't hot, I wanted to go home.

Do you know it too, that feeling in the changing room, when you're moving as quickly as you can? Putting your clothes back on, preferably never to be taken off again, hoping nobody will see you, your unsuitable body, your inability to conform. I had no other depictions, no images of women to model what I needed. Not just physically, but more generally as well. I was fifteen years old and giving myself as many orgasms as I could, but I tried not to look at myself; back then I hated catching so much as a glimpse of my body. I was fifteen years old and I wanted to find words, I wanted to speak, but I found them so rarely, the words.

And then, dancing with you, Nora. With you so many things became so easy, did you know that? When we were together, that heaviness was barely there at all, and I felt as though you understood me. You understand even what I do not say.

And then Vural, looking at his body, always only at his. The trim stomach, the youthful arms. With him the words came easily, quite uninhibited; and he never had a bad word to say about my body, and so I could forget it all a little.

And then Phil, how safe I feel with him, how cared-for. He doesn't judge, he doesn't judge my body. With him I have never felt under scrutiny I think he listens more than he sees, and he likes to listen to me, I have noticed that.

And then Dennis. I take off my pullover, take off my shirt. He contemplates me. I am aware of the smallness of my breasts, but also of the way they hum, vibrate, before I even touch them, or he touches them. I take off my skirt, my leggings. I'm in my underwear.

I feel the softness of my legs. I am more naked than I have ever been, and I weep. And Dennis is still sitting before me, regarding me, regarding my thighs, my feet. He touches them. His hands glide up my legs and come to rest on the bones of my hips. I strip off my knickers and he looks at my vulva. I can feel how wet I am, large and full, and although I sense Dennis's gaze all at once I just let go, I let it be, and that night it is as though I feel myself for the first time, the first time ever — in my entirety. And with sensation comes speech, from somewhere deep down, from places that are hidden.

And now here I lie, almost thirty years of age, and I am so open. What woman am I today?

I don't know exactly what it will be, but I think that I have more to tell you, more to show you. I think there's still so much we've never told each other, and I want to change that.

WHAT CONCERNS US

LAURA VOGT

TRANSLATED BY CAROLINE WAIGHT

HÉ/OïSE

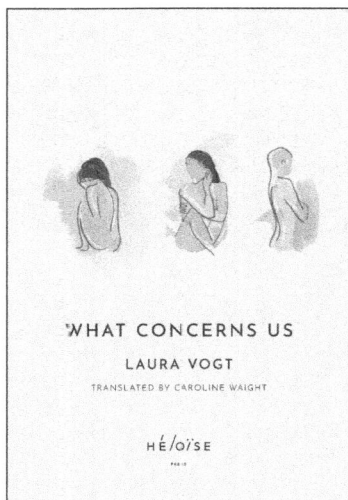

ISBN: 9781739751517

Rahel and Fenna grew up in an all-female household with their mother and her female partner. Now Rahel strives to reproduce the traditional family unit but she is haunted by an unsettling pregnancy, postnatal depression, and compulsive breastfeeding, while having mixed feelings about her singing career. Meanwhile, Fenna wonders whether she consented to the intercourse with Luc which left her pregnant. *What Concerns Us* is a punchy contemporary read that scrutinises gender roles within our society, examining what it means to be a mother, the nature of femininity, as well as how to remain independent in different types of relationship.

'A beautiful examination of female interiority. Vogt is not afraid to ask difficult questions. In what ways does motherhood bring us to our limits? What are the consequences of believing a child doesn't need a father?'

ELIZABETH MCNEILL, *Chicago Review of Books*